SPANIEL in a STOCKING

SPANIEL in a STOCKING

by Ben M. Baglio

SCHOLASTIC INC.

New York Toronto London Auckland Sydney
Mexico City New Delhi Hong Kong Buenos Aires

ISBN-13: 978-0-439-871181
ISBN-10: 0-439-87118-2

12 11 10 9 8 7 6 5 4   7 8 9 10 11/0

Printed in the U.S.A.   40
First Scholastic printing, November 2006

Special thanks to Lucy Courtenay

SPANIEL in a
STOCKING

One

". . . So, much of the North, particularly the Yorkshire moors, can expect heavy snowfall over the next few days." The TV weatherperson beamed out of the small screen, her blond hair swinging jauntily on her shoulders. "Perhaps we'll have a white Christmas after all! Now it's back to Sally in the studio."

"Did you hear that?" Mandy Hope poked her best friend, James Hunter, in the ribs. "It's going to snow!"

James nodded enthusiastically. "We can go sledding on my dad's toboggan! He got it down from the attic last week and I've been helping him polish the wooden runners with this special oil to make it extra fast."

1

"I bet it's not as fast as my plastic sled," Mandy argued.

James's eyes gleamed. "We'll have to have a race," he announced.

Dr. Emily Hope came into the living room, tucking her curly red hair behind her ears. "TV off, please," she said. "The committee will be here at any moment."

Mandy jumped off the sofa and flicked off the television. "We're going to have a white Christmas, Mom! They just said so!"

"Really?" Dr. Emily looked delighted. "Somehow snow makes everything feel more festive, doesn't it?" She straightened a stack of magazines on the coffee table and then went on more seriously, "but we don't want to get snowed in for too long. That would cause all kinds of problems."

"But think how pretty Welford will look!" Mandy said persuasively. "Snow on the roofs, and the fields all soft and white and fat looking. Carols with snow falling outside the window!"

Dr. Emily shook her head. "Looking picturesque isn't much use when the roads are icy and dangerous, and we have to shovel snow away from the doorstep every morning. Think of the sick animals who might not get to the clinic!"

Mandy's parents ran Animal Ark, a veterinary clinic

attached to their old stone cottage in the village of Welford. Mandy couldn't imagine living anywhere more perfect. Her whole life revolved around animals — healthy, sick, or in trouble — and she'd always known that she would be a vet when she grew up.

Mandy went over to the living-room window and peered outside. "Maybe the snow will be deep enough to sled on, but not deep enough to stop people from bringing their animals to the clinic," she suggested hopefully.

Her mom smiled. "It's a nice idea, but unfortunately snow isn't something you can order by the inch!"

Mandy narrowed her eyes to peer into the half-light outside. "James, quick!" she called. "Is that a snowflake?"

"No," said James, coming over to stand beside her. "It's just a smudge on your windowpane, Mandy."

"Oh." Mandy turned away from the window. "Well, it'll snow soon, won't it? And we can have snowball fights and make snow angels and . . ."

". . . get cold feet inside your snow boots," Dr. Adam Hope finished for her as he ducked through the living-room door. He took off his woolen hat and rubbed at his beard. "Brrr, it's cold out there. Hello, Blackie."

Blackie, James's black Labrador, had rushed up to

Dr. Adam and was banging his tail against his legs in delight.

"Is the rest of the Christmas Dance Committee with you, Adam?" Dr. Emily asked. "We've got tons of stuff to figure out, and the dance is only six days from now!"

"You're always so disorganized, Mom!" Mandy teased, flipping her dark blond hair out of her eyes. "You've booked the hall, haven't you?"

Welford's annual Christmas Eve Dance in the village hall was a very popular event, but this year everyone on the Dance Committee had been so busy that some things had been left to the last minute.

"Yes, but that's about the only thing we have managed to do." Dr. Emily sighed.

"I think the missing committee members are just coming up the driveway," said Dr. Adam, who was looking out the window. "It looks as if my mother's bringing enough mince pies to last a three-month siege."

"Just as well, if we're going to get as much snow as they say," said Dr. Emily.

"What's the matter with everyone?" Mandy exclaimed. "Snow's fun, too, you know."

Mandy's mom relented. "I know, Mandy," she said. "It looks gorgeous. Come on, help me get the refreshments together. The others will be here at any moment."

On cue, Grandma Hope appeared at the kitchen door. She handed Mandy three Tupperware boxes. "The top two are mince pies, and the bottom one is chocolate chip cookies," she advised, unwinding her long red scarf and smoothing down her neat gray hair. "Ooh, it's nice to get out of the wind."

"You like snow, don't you, Gran?" Mandy said hopefully. She opened the boxes and began piling the mince pies and cookies onto plates.

"As long as I can admire it from somewhere nice and warm with a hot cup of tea in my hand," said Dorothy Hope, "then I like it very much." She turned around as two more people entered the kitchen. "Hello, Julian — hello, Sara!" she called. "Full of ideas for this year's Christmas dance, I hope?"

"Evening, Dorothy." Julian Hardy, the dark-haired landlord from the Fox and Goose, grinned. "Evening, Mandy."

"Hello everyone," Sara, Julian Hardy's petite blond wife said, smiling. Her nose was bright red from the cold.

"Come through to the living room," Mandy urged. "It's even warmer in there. Hey, Sara, do you like snow?"

"Of course!" said Sara. Mandy beamed at her.

Blackie was stretching his head up to sniff at the plates on the table. Mandy put them up out of his reach,

and James held him by the collar to stop him from following the others into the living room. Then James
squeezed through the door after Mandy, leaving Blackie
alone in the kitchen.

"OK, let's get started," said Dr. Emily, when Mandy
had poured refreshments for everyone and they had all
settled down with a mince pie. "We still haven't agreed
on the music. Does anyone have any thoughts?"

"How about some nice jazz?" suggested Mandy's
grandfather, Tom Hope. He grabbed Mandy's grandmother by the hand and pulled her, laughing, out of her
seat. "Come on, Dorothy, let's show them how it used to
be done!"

"It looks pretty complicated," Mandy said doubtfully,
watching her grandparents twirl around the room. "This
is a dance, Grandad, not the ballet. We need music that
everyone can dance to!"

"We'll take a vote," Dr. Emily said diplomatically. "All
those in favor of jazz?"

Tom Hope raised his hand. A little out of breath,
Mandy's grandmother put up her hand as well.

"Jazz was never really my thing," said Julian Hardy
apologetically.

"Me, neither," Sara Hardy added.

Mandy's parents shook their heads as well. "Too bad,

Mom," Dr. Adam sympathized. "You and Dad have been outvoted."

Clearly annoyed at being left out in the kitchen, Blackie whined and scratched at the door.

"Sorry, Blackie," Dr. Emily called. "Your vote doesn't count."

Mandy grinned, picturing Blackie trotting around the village hall on his back legs.

"I heard about this DJ named Jay Burton who lives in Walton," said James, blushing. "He was going to do a party for one of my friends at school, but it got canceled because they're going away for Christmas instead. Jay is very popular, but if we call him right now he might still be available."

"What kind of music does he play?" asked Mrs. Hardy.

"A real mix, I hear," said James. "Old stuff, Christmas stuff, new stuff. I've got his number, if you want it."

"Take a vote?" Dr. Emily suggested, looking around the table.

Seven hands went up.

"Don't worry, he'll probably have some old songs like *White Christmas*, too," James said encouragingly to Mandy's grandfather.

"Hey, we're not too old for modern music!" Tom Hope protested. "We'll dance to anything, won't we, Dorothy?"

James produced the DJ's number on a scrap of paper from his pocket and Dr. Emily went out of the room to make the call.

As the rest of the committee discussed ticket prices, Mandy heard a suspicious drumming sound down by her chair. She looked down. Blackie was skulking by the coffee table, beating his tail nervously.

"What's Blackie doing in here?" said Mandy's dad, noticing him, too.

"He must've come in when Mom went out to the kitchen," Mandy guessed.

Blackie backed away from the coffee table, leaving a suspicious trail of crumbs in his wake.

James gasped. "He's eaten a mince pie!"

Blackie looked guilty as everyone leaped out of their seats. Sure enough, one of the plates on the coffee table was empty except for a few crumbs of crust.

"He's eaten a whole plateful!" Dorothy Hope exclaimed. "My, that'll give him a stomachache!"

Blackie whined.

"I think he's going to be sick," Mandy said anxiously. Blackie whined again and crouched down with his tail clamped to his haunches.

Dr. Adam bent down and gave him a quick examination, feeling his tummy and checking his eyelids and heart rate. "Good thing the cookies were out of his reach," he said. "Chocolate isn't good for dogs because it contains a chemical called theobromine, which is poisonous to them in large enough quantities. As it is, he's just stuffed himself with pastry and mincemeat. A quiet rest will cure it. Come on, you greedy dog! Plenty of water and no food until tomorrow, I think."

James and Mandy followed Dr. Adam and Blackie out of the living room. As they passed through the kitchen, Dr. Emily glanced up from her phone call and frowned inquiringly at them. *Tell you later*, Mandy mouthed.

The spacious, cage-lined residential unit at the back of the clinic was empty except for a cat sleeping off the anesthetic from a minor operation. As Christmas approached, Mandy's parents tried to ensure all pets were at home with their owners to enjoy the holiday.

"In you go." Dr. Adam put Blackie in a corner cage while Mandy got a bowl of water. Blackie blinked mournfully up at them. He didn't even seem interested in the sleeping cat.

"This is the best place for you," James told him. "I'll come and see you later, don't worry."

Mandy switched off the light as they left the unit, hoping Blackie would get some sleep in the peaceful dark.

"Good news, everyone," said Dr. Emily, following Mandy, James, and her husband back into the living room. "Jay Burton can do our dance!"

Everyone cheered.

The second item on the agenda was decorating the hall.

"I can make a mistletoe ball for the middle of the dance floor," Grandpa Hope offered. "I'll tie it up with ivy and holly. All the red and white berries will look fantastic against the dark green leaves."

"And I'm sure we've got plenty of festive-colored garland," said Mr. Hardy.

"We could drape the walls in white and silver," Mandy suggested, her mind still full of thoughts of snow. "It would look like an ice cave!"

"That's a lovely idea," said Dr. Emily.

"Let's hope that's the only ice we see," added her grandfather.

Mandy sighed. Grown-ups just didn't *get* it. As the agenda moved on to less exciting things like restrooms and car parking, she let her mind wander to all the exciting things she and James could do if it snowed. They could make a Santa-styled snowman — or get some of those icicle lights to hang off the house and reflect all the *real* icicles — or . . .

"Earth to Mandy," said Dr. Emily. "Are you still with us?"

"Hmm?"

"Are you and James happy to deal with the publicity?"

asked Mandy's mom, sounding as if she'd already asked the question once. "We'll need posters and also flyers to put in people's mailboxes."

"Definitely," Mandy said. She'd already had an idea for the posters.

"Count me in," James added.

Dr. Emily consulted the agenda one last time. "Well, that covers everything," she said. "Thanks for coming, everyone."

As Mandy's mom opened the door to usher out their guests, Mandy and James peered hopefully at the black sky. There was no sign of snow, but there was a telltale bite in the air that promised snow very soon.

"Can James stay and work on the poster with me now?" Mandy asked her mother as soon as the last committee member had gone. "Like you said, Mom, there's only six days to go until the dance!"

"It's kind of late," said Dr. Emily. "But I'll call your mother and ask her, James."

"Thanks, Dr. Emily," said James. "We'll try not to be too long!"

"Let's check on Blackie first," Mandy said, towing James toward the unit, "and then we can go up to my computer. I've got a fantastic idea for the posters."

Blackie thumped his tail against the side of his cage as Mandy and James entered the residential unit. His water bowl was half empty, so Mandy filled it up. He definitely looked brighter, especially when Mandy and James opened his cage and made a fuss over him, but they left him in the unit while they headed upstairs to make the posters.

"So, what's your idea?" asked James.

"A silver-and-white color scheme, with big red letters," Mandy replied. "We can add some silver glitter for a final, wintry touch. What do you think?"

"Sounds great! And we can make the writing look like icicles," James said enthusiastically.

They switched on Mandy's computer and got to work.

"There," Mandy said a half hour later, hitting the SAVE button with satisfaction. "I'll ask Mom if we can print some of these on the color printer." She opened her desk drawer and rummaged around for the silver glitter glue she'd used to make her Christmas cards.

"Look," James gasped, pointing to the window. "Snow!"

Mandy leaped out of the chair as if she'd been stung. She and James pressed their noses to the glass and watched the big fluffy flakes tumbling from the sky. The first flakes were melting as soon as they touched the ground, but soon there was a sprinkling of white powder on the fields and walls and trees all around.

"Mom!" Mandy yelled, running downstairs with James close behind. "It's snowing!"

"Slow down!" Dr. Emily protested as they pelted into the kitchen.

Mandy seized her mom's hands and pulled her around in a little dance. "I won't be able to sleep tonight," she said, laughing. "It's too exciting!"

Dr. Emily gently pulled her hands away. "I thought you'd grown out of Christmas insomnia when you were four," she teased.

Mandy suddenly remembered the posters. "Can we print our posters on the clinic's color printer?" she asked. "We've only got to add the glitter and then they're done. Oh, and can we laminate them, too? Otherwise the snow might ruin them."

Dr. Emily raised her eyebrows. "That's the first negative thing you've said about the snow, Mandy."

"First and only," Mandy promised. "So, can we? Please, Mom!"

Twenty minutes later, the posters and flyers were printed, and after some liberal glitter gluing, the posters were ready for the laminating machine. Mandy held up the first poster to the light, where the glitter sparkled like tiny stars.

"James!" Dr. Emily called. "Your mom's here!"

"I'll meet you tomorrow at nine, outside the Fox and Goose," Mandy suggested, as James ran to get Blackie and find his coat. "We'll put up the posters and hand out the flyers then."

As Mandy headed up to bed, she felt a hopeful shiver as she thought of the pristine white snow that would be waiting outside for her in the morning. It was going to feel like Christmas had arrived early!

Two

As soon as Mandy woke up, she ran to the window and pulled back the drapes.

"Oh," she said, crestfallen.

There was only a very thin covering of snow, as if someone had lightly brushed the ground and trees with confectioner's sugar. Higher up on the tops of the hills, the snow was a little deeper, but in the Hopes' backyard, dark green blades of grass could be seen clearly. The sky still looked gray and heavy, but it wasn't snowing now.

Dr. Emily came into Mandy's bedroom. "Are you disappointed, sweetie?" she said sympathetically.

15

"Yes, a little," Mandy admitted.

"Don't be," said her mom. "There's more snow forecast for later today. There's oatmeal downstairs, if that's any consolation."

Mandy pulled on her clothes and headed downstairs. She started to feel better as she poured a dollop of cream on her warm oatmeal and sprinkled some crusty brown sugar on the top. Then, resting her chin on her hand, she stared out of the window at the sky, willing the snow to fall.

"What time are you meeting James?" Dr. Emily asked.

"Nine o'clock," Mandy replied, stirring her oatmeal.

"Make sure you wrap up warmly," her mother warned. "Two pairs of socks inside your boots, too."

After breakfast, Mandy folded the flyers and rolled up the laminated posters very carefully before loading them into her backpack.

"Where are you going to put the posters?" Dr. Emily asked, standing in the door of the clinic as Mandy put on her coat.

"One on Mrs. McFarlane's board at the post office, one at the Fox and Goose, one on the church bulletin board, and one at the village hall," Mandy answered promptly.

"And you're going to put the flyers in people's mailboxes?"

Mandy nodded. "We'll knock on a few doors, too, in case people don't come out to see the posters," she said. "I'd better go, Mom. It's a quarter to nine."

She headed down to the shed to get her bike. The wind whistled around her head, trying to blow down the neck of her coat. Shivering, she pulled up her collar and tied her scarf more tightly. Her mom had been right about the cold.

As she pedaled into the village, taking care to avoid the shiny patches of ice, Mandy glanced up at the sky again. Were there a few more snow clouds than there had been at breakfast?

"I'm glad you're not late," James greeted her, stamping his feet. "I thought I was going to freeze on the spot." Beside him, Blackie thumped his tail in agreement.

Mandy locked up her bike outside the inn, then pulled the first poster out of her bag and fixed it to the Fox and Goose bulletin board. The red letters shone out like beacons, and the glitter sparkled like frost.

"It looks terrific," said James, stepping back to admire the poster. "Oops!"

His feet skidded sideways on a frozen puddle. Mandy seized his arm and pulled him upright. "Not very graceful," she teased. "I don't think your style would impress many ice-skating judges!"

They put another poster on the church bulletin board

and one on the village hall next door. Then they came to the post office and general store, where they wanted to leave a poster in the window. Grateful to get into the warmth, Mandy stamped her feet on the doormat and pulled off her hat.

"Morning, Mrs. McFarlane!" she called.

Mrs. McFarlane the store owner and postmistress rushed out of her office but when she saw Mandy and James her face seemed to fall. "Oh," she said. "Good morning, you two."

"Are we bad news?" James joked, rubbing his misted-up glasses on his scarf. "We've brought a poster for the Christmas dance. Can we put it in the window?"

Mrs. McFarlane didn't seem to be listening; instead, she was peering out the frosty window.

"Mrs. McFarlane?" Mandy prompted. "Is everything all right?"

"Hmm?" Mrs. McFarlane turned around. "Oh, yes, everything's fine, dear. I'm just expecting something this morning."

"What?" Mandy asked, pricking up her ears.

Mrs. McFarlane tapped the side of her nose, warning Mandy not to be too curious. "You'll find out soon enough." She smiled. "Of course you can put up a poster for the Christmas dance. There should be just enough room next to the ad for the Farmers' Market."

Mandy used strips of sticky tape to fix the poster on the window so that people would be able to see it from outside. "Are you coming, Mrs. McFarlane?" she asked.

Mrs. McFarlane was looking out the window again. "Mr. McFarlane and I are a little old for dances," she said vaguely. "But we'll see."

Blackie, who had been tied outside the post office, was very pleased to see Mandy and James when they headed into the cold again.

"Mrs. McFarlane was acting weird," Mandy commented as James bent down to untie Blackie's leash.

"She's probably expecting a Christmas present in the mail," James said, straightening up. "Look out for that patch of ice, Mandy."

Mandy narrowed her eyes, concentrating hard. Then she put one foot at the edge of the large frozen puddle and pushed off with the other, so that she slid gracefully all the way to the far end.

"Very nice!" James declared. "Come on. We've still got all those flyers to deliver."

They decided to start at the far end of the village and work their way back toward Animal Ark. The sky was definitely looking heavier now, and Mandy felt sure they would see snowflakes at any moment. Finally, they reached the last road in the village, where the little gray stone houses sat close to the sweeping fields. There was a funky-looking Christmas wreath on the front door of the last house, made of tinsel and tiny gold apples. Whoever lived here clearly had some very creative ideas about decorations!

Mandy pulled a flyer out of her backpack and banged the door knocker twice.

The door was opened by a bored-looking girl of about eighteen, with long dark hair and a brightly colored wool sweater with an unusual design that reminded Mandy of a winding country road. To Mandy's delight, a chubby black cocker spaniel also appeared, wagging its tail furiously.

"What a gorgeous dog!" Mandy exclaimed, bending down to pet the dog. The spaniel, whose black fur was flecked with gray on its chest and muzzle, wagged its tail even harder and made a stiff-legged attempt to jump up and lick Mandy's nose.

"Get down, Tarka!" the girl said impatiently. "Sorry," she added to Mandy and James. "She hasn't had a walk today. Tarka! Get out of the way! Uh, can I help you?"

Mandy straightened up. "I'm Mandy Hope," she said. "And this is my friend James Hunter. We're delivering flyers for the Welford Christmas dance."

The girl took the flyer Mandy was offering and studied it. "Sounds OK," she said, putting the flyer on the hall table. "Oh, for goodness sake, Tarka," she snapped as the spaniel tried to launch itself at Mandy again. "Stop that silly jumping and slobbering!"

Something about the stiff-legged way in which the spaniel was moving rang a warning bell in Mandy's mind. Thoughtfully, she crouched down and ran a hand down the dog's back legs. "I don't mind her being playful," she assured the girl. "I love dogs. My parents run Animal Ark."

The girl looked blank.

"The veterinary clinic?" Mandy prompted.

"Oh, right," said the girl. "It's Mom's dog, so she deals with stuff like that. Did you want anything else?"

The spaniel tried to jump up again and landed awkwardly, almost toppling over.

"Sit *down*, Tarka." The girl sighed. "You're so annoying sometimes."

The spaniel sat. Curiously, it splayed out its legs behind itself like a frog, rather than tucking them neatly under its body.

"Does she always sit like that?" Mandy asked.

The girl looked down. "I guess so. Mom would know. Like I said, Tarka's Mom's dog. I just got back from college last week."

Mandy wanted a closer look at the spaniel. "What are you studying?" she asked the girl, edging toward the open door.

"Theater design," said the girl. "Right now, I'm halfway through a big project that involves building a scaled-down version of a famous theater set."

"That sounds really interesting!" Mandy exclaimed, meaning it. "Do you mind if we come in? I'd love to see your project."

"Sure." The girl smiled for the first time. "I'm Lauren, by the way," she said. "So you like the theater?"

"I don't know much about it," Mandy admitted. "But we go to the Christmas show in Walton almost every year."

The hall was drafty, but the low-ceilinged living room was cozy. As they followed Lauren inside, Mandy noticed brightly colored posters on the walls advertising concerts, in between colorful wall drapes of tie-dyed cotton. Tarka weaved through their legs, sniffing at the Blackie smells on James's jeans. James kept Blackie on a short leash so he didn't jump around and knock over any of the ornaments that dotted every surface in the room.

"Your house is amazing," Mandy remarked, ducking her head as she and James followed Lauren into the sitting room. "It feels like a big tent."

"That's my mom's fault," Lauren replied, though she was smiling. "She sings in a band and she's spent so many years living in tents at music festivals that she likes her home that way, too. Well, here's the project."

She pointed to a table underneath the window where there was a complicated-looking arrangement of wire, fabric, and sheets of colored card stock. Mandy went closer, and gasped.

The theater was perfect in every detail. The backdrop was molded from silver gauze and columns of twisted silver wire circled the stage. Sparkly snowflakes, each one barely bigger than the real thing, hung from the ceiling.

"It's a set for the *Snow Queen*," Lauren explained. "You know, the Hans Christian Andersen story? This is the Snow Queen's palace."

"It's gorgeous," Mandy breathed.

"I feel cold just looking at it," James agreed, bending down next to Mandy.

Tarka had paused to touch noses with Blackie, but now she bounded around the sofa as if she wanted Mandy to play with her.

"Tarka!" Lauren exclaimed as the spaniel lurched into the Christmas tree. Two crystal baubles fell from the branches and rolled across the room. "She knocked over my set yesterday and nearly ruined it! She's been driving me crazy all week."

Mandy reached over and tickled Tarka's speckled belly. Personally, she thought Lauren was being a bit harsh. Tarka just wanted some attention. The spaniel squirmed with delight as Mandy ran her hand down the dog's hind legs. "She's a bit stiff," she remarked to Lauren. "My dad might be able to prescribe something to help. Has your mom brought her to Animal Ark lately?"

Lauren shrugged. "I've been at college, so I don't know. And Mom's visiting Grandpa today, so I can't ask her. Did you want anything else? I've got to get back to work." She glared at the spaniel. "It would be almost finished by now if it wasn't for Tarka."

"So, do you think you'll come to the dance?" James prompted, as Lauren shooed Tarka out of the living room and opened the front door for them.

"Don't think so," said Lauren. "I don't know anyone

around here, so it wouldn't be much fun. Thanks for the flyer, anyway."

Outside, some small flakes were twirling out of the sky. It wasn't enough for the blankets of snow Mandy wanted, but it was a start. She gave Tarka a final pat. The spaniel looked up at her with beseeching brown eyes.

"Listen, does Tarka —" Mandy began.

"See you around," Lauren said with a brief smile, and shut the door.

Mandy stared thoughtfully at the wreath of gold apples on Lauren's front door. She had a nasty feeling she knew what Tarka's problem was. And if Lauren didn't get her mom to bring the spaniel into the Animal Ark very soon, it was going to get a lot worse.

Three

"Lauren really should come to the dance," said James. "It would help her to make friends in the village." Blackie pulled and tugged at his leash as they made their way toward the village green. "Mandy? Are you listening?"

"Hmm?" Mandy blinked at James. "Sorry, I was miles away."

"Doesn't matter," James said. "What's bugging you?"

"Tarka," Mandy confessed. "Lauren's mom really needs to bring her into the clinic so my mom or dad can take a look at her legs."

"She's probably just old," James reasoned, sticking

another flyer in a mailbox. "My grandparents used to have a dog with arthritis and he got very stiff, too."

"I don't know," Mandy said. "I think there's more to it than that. I want to get back to Animal Ark and talk to Mom or Dad. We've done more than half the village. Do you mind doing the rest on your own?"

"No," said James. "I can see you're really worried about Tarka."

"Thanks." Mandy gratefully handed her backpack to him. "I'll call you later."

The snow was falling more heavily now, but Mandy's thoughts were too full of Tarka to notice. She pedaled as fast as she dared through the flurry of snowflakes, dropped her bike in the garage, and ran inside.

Jean Knox, the Animal Ark receptionist, looked up as Mandy burst through the clinic door. No one was in the waiting room.

"Hi, Jean," said Mandy in a rush. "Are Mom and Dad busy?"

"Your dad's next patient is in about ten minutes," said Jean, consulting the appointment book. "He's probably in the kitchen."

"Thanks!" Mandy hurried through the adjoining door into the kitchen.

Dr. Adam looked up guiltily from a plate of half-eaten mince pies.

"Honestly, Dad," Mandy said, distracted from thoughts of Tarka for a moment, "you're as bad as Blackie!"

"It's your grandmother's fault," said Dr. Adam. "She makes the best mince pies in Yorkshire. What have you been up to this morning?"

"Well, we put up our posters around the village," Mandy began. "But Dad —"

"Did you put one up in the post office?" Dr. Adam interrupted. "Did Mrs. McFarlane mention a package for me?"

"We did go to the post office, but Mrs. McFarlane didn't say anything. What are you expecting?"

"Just some supplies," he replied. He looked past Mandy. "Where's James? Did you come back alone?"

Mandy quickly told him about Lauren and Tarka. "I think Tarka's got hip dysplasia," she finished.

Dr. Adam raised his eyebrows. "That's a pretty serious diagnosis," he said. "What makes you so sure?"

Mandy reached for a mince pie while she thought. "I didn't think it was full-blown arthritis," she said at last, "because Tarka didn't seem to be in huge amounts of pain. She just acted clumsy, as if her back legs weren't working correctly. She sat with her legs out behind her, like sitting any other way would be uncomfortable. She was fat, too, and overweight dogs can develop problems with their hips, can't they? I just got a bad feeling, Dad. If you don't catch hip dysplasia soon, it can worsen quickly, can't it?"

Dr. Adam nodded. "The degeneration of the hip socket is quite common in medium to large breeds like spaniels," he said. "Sometimes it's a result of diet, or overexercise on young puppy bones, but it's usually inherited. Basically, it means Tarka's leg bones don't fit into the hip socket properly, which makes it tricky for her to move around. I'd recommend something like glucosamine to help repair the damaged cartilage, as well as plenty of gentle exercise. But the only way you can diagnose hip dysplasia for sure is with an X-ray. Did Lauren's mother say she'd bring Tarka in?"

"Lauren's mom wasn't there," Mandy said. "And I don't think Lauren was listening when I asked her to tell her mom to bring Tarka into the clinic. Can't you write them a letter, telling them to come in?"

"You can't force a dog owner to bring their pet to a vet," Dr. Adam said. "And remember, it could be a completely different problem. Did you see where Tarka slept?"

Mandy tried to remember. "I think I saw a dog bed in the hall, just inside the front door."

"A drafty hallway could be making her stiffness

worse," Dr. Adam said. "Tarka's getting old, and this weather doesn't help. That might be all there is to it."

Jean Knox put her head around the kitchen door. "Your next patient is here, Dr. Adam," she said.

Dr. Adam looked regretfully at the last mince pie. "I'll be right out," he promised Jean. "Listen," he said, turning back to Mandy, "try not to worry, OK? I'll see you later."

The snow fell thicker and thicker through the rest of the morning. Mandy's superfast sled was propped up in the porch, but with her mind full of Tarka, she couldn't work up any enthusiasm for a race.

She called James after lunch.

"What did your dad say about Tarka?" James asked, as if he hadn't been thinking about the snow much, either.

"He can't be sure without seeing Tarka and taking an X-ray," Mandy said. "But I know there's a problem, James. I just *know* it."

"We should drop around to Lauren's house later and see if we can catch her mom," James suggested.

"Maybe," Mandy agreed. "Listen, James, thanks for delivering the rest of the flyers. I owe you a big favor!"

"Just make my Christmas present extra special this year," James joked before he put the phone down.

Christmas presents! Mandy suddenly remembered that she and her mom were supposed to go shopping that afternoon in Walton. She ran upstairs to find her Christmas list. Thick hiking socks from the outdoor store for Dad; her mom's special rose soap; a cookbook for her grandmother; and a dibble, a gardening tool, for her grandfather. Mandy grabbed a pen and added a few things: a bag of treats for any animals stuck in the residential unit over Christmas; the latest book of soccer statistics for James; one of those squeaky toys she'd seen in the Walton pet store for Blackie; and catnip toys for James's cat, Eric, and her grandparents' cat, Smoky.

"We'd better go if we want to beat the weather, Mandy!" Dr. Emily called.

Stuffing the list in her jeans pocket, Mandy ran downstairs.

"It's going to be freezing out there," her mom warned, as Mandy wriggled into her coat. "I don't think we should stay out too long. I don't like the look of this snow."

"Mom!" Mandy complained. "All you do is moan about the snow. It's fantastic!"

The hills and fields were looking gorgeous now, as the snow blanketed all the rough parts and made everything look like frosting on a Christmas cake. Mandy followed her mom to the car, her spirits lightening as

she watched the snowflakes cascading from the heavy
sky. She tried to catch a snowflake on her tongue, then
hopped into the backseat.

It was slow going out of the village. Several cars
crawled in front of them and it was difficult to see more
than twenty yards ahead. As they climbed out of the val-
ley, the traffic slowed down even more and visibility got
steadily worse until Dr. Emily was forced to turn on her
headlights.

"Do you think Dad wants hiking socks for Christmas?" Mandy asked, consulting her list.

"A vet can never have enough thick socks," said Dr. Emily as she steered carefully around a snowdrift that curled under the hedge like a frozen wave. "I . . . oh . . ."

Mandy felt the car wobble out of control. Very slowly, it slid sideways — and with a gentle crunch, she felt the front wheel slip into the shallow ditch at the side of the road. The car lurched forward and came to a halt.

Dr. Emily made an exasperated noise. "Looks like we stop here, Mandy." She sighed, peering out of the snowy windshield. "I don't think we've damaged the car, but we're really stuck. Oh, thank goodness! Julian Hardy's behind us."

Mandy twisted around and watched as Mr. Hardy stopped his car and hurried over. He waved a short length of tow rope at them. "Don't worry, I'll have you out of there in no time."

Other cars crawled past them at a snail's pace as Mandy and her mom helped Mr. Hardy attach the tow rope and pull the car out of the ditch. After thanking him profusely, Dr. Emily ushered Mandy back to the car. Mandy brushed at the snowflakes on her shoulders and her hair. She was beginning to see what her mom meant about the snow.

They crept a little farther up the hill. But flashing police lights ahead warned of more problems.

Mandy's mom rolled down the car window. "What's happening, officer?"

"Sorry to inconvenience you, ma'am," said the policeman, "but we're closing the road."

Mandy gasped. Closing the road? How were they going to get to Walton?

"I understand," Dr. Emily said. "It's not an urgent journey."

"It *is* urgent," Mandy hissed. "I haven't got any Christmas presents yet!"

"Sorry, miss," said the policeman. "The snow might be cleared away in a couple of days. Maybe you can do your shopping then." He stood up and called to the car behind. "Turn around, please, sir! This road is closed!"

"Sorry, Mandy," said Dr. Emily, putting the car into reverse and turning around very slowly.

"What about our Christmas shopping?" Mandy asked in dismay.

Dr. Emily shook her head. "It looks like we'll have to get creative this year and make do with what we can find at home."

Impossibly, the snow seemed to be even heavier now. Visibility was almost zero, and the scenic hills and fields had vanished behind a wall of snow and mist. Even with

their headlights on high and the wipers working over-
time, it was a slow and painful crawl back to Welford.
Mandy stared at her Christmas list, then crumpled it up
and stuffed it back in her pocket.

What would she give everyone for Christmas now?

Four

Mandy opened her eyes. Her bedroom was filled with a strange, white light. Was it morning already? Yawning and screwing up her eyes, she got out of bed, pulled open the drapes — and gasped.

Every flake of yesterday's snow had settled, burying every inch of landscape from the stone walls around the fields to the bare branches of the trees. Peering down at the lawn, Mandy spotted neat little bird footprints hopping across the fluffy whiteness. It was a perfect winter wonderland!

The unpleasant drive to Walton the day before was forgotten as Mandy grabbed her robe and charged downstairs. Flinging open the back door, she took a gulp of pure icy air and stared at the picture-postcard scene before her.

"Please tell me you're not going outside in bare feet." Dr. Emily put her arm around Mandy's shoulders, and together they stared out the door.

"It's so beautiful," Mandy whispered. Her heart leaped as she thought of the sledding race she could have with James today.

Dr. Emily looked up at the sky, which was still dark and gray. "There's more snow forecast," she said. "At this rate, we'll be snowed in by the evening."

Mandy dipped her bare toe in a nearby patch of crystal white snow and drew a little circle. The snow sparkled like diamonds, and the tip of her toe turned bright pink with cold.

"I've got to get to the post office before the clinic opens this morning," said Dr. Adam, coming into the kitchen. "To, uh, pick up my supplies."

"That's assuming the mail has gotten through," Dr. Emily pointed out.

Mandy thought of Mrs. McFarlane and yesterday's delivery. Now was her chance to find out what the postmistress had been waiting for. "I'll go, Dad," she offered.

Dr. Adam looked startled. "No, that's all right, Mandy. . . ."

Mandy went over and kissed her dad on the head. "It's no trouble," she said.

"Wait —" Dr. Adam began. But Mandy was already running upstairs to find her warmest clothes.

As soon as Mandy had washed and dressed, she called James.

"I'm going to the post office for Dad this morning," she told him. "Want to come? Mrs. McFarlane's delivery might have arrived yesterday. I'm dying to see what it is!"

"Maybe it's a snowmobile," James joked. "OK. I'll see you outside the Fox and Goose in twenty minutes."

"Mandy, you really don't have to get my package," said Dr. Adam, as soon as Mandy came back into the kitchen.

"Stop worrying, Dad," she said, pulling on her boots and selecting a fluffy hat from the coat stand. "Whatever it is, I won't drop it in any snowdrifts, I promise."

"OK," said Dr. Adam reluctantly. "You're not planning on taking your bike, are you? The road's really treacherous out there. You'd be better off walking."

Mandy thought of all the ice patches there might be between Animal Ark and the village, and how she could practice sliding on them all. "Fine," she said, grabbing a piece of toast. "See you later!"

She dashed outside, her boots leaving a line of deep prints in the snow. The air had a kind of soft thickness that stung Mandy's throat with its icy bite. She aimed carefully at the first length of really hard ice she could see and took a run at it. As soon as her feet touched it, they shot away from underneath her.

"Oops . . ." Picking herself up and dusting off her jeans, Mandy frowned at the ice. Perhaps she should try a better sliding angle next time.

She made her way into the village by jumping from one ice patch to another, imagining herself on a snowy ice rink in a pair of white ice skates and a sparkling costume. As she approached the Fox and Goose, she tried a pirouette — and bumped smack into James.

"Glad we ran into each other like this," she joked, helping James to his feet. "Hi, Blackie. How about playing in the snow?"

Blackie put his head on one side, looking a little uncertain.

"He's a little spooked by the snow," James told Mandy, brushing his coat down and straightening his glasses, which were misted up with the cold. "Nothing looks or smells the same."

Blackie wagged his tail forlornly, and Mandy stroked him. "Poor old boy," she said. "Never mind. Once you've chased a few snowballs, I'm sure you'll like it more."

At that moment, a clump of snow smacked between her shoulder blades, and Mandy whirled around.

James was grinning at her, already shaping the next snowball in his gloved hands. "Just getting you back for knocking me over!"

"That's it!" Mandy scooped up a handful of snow and flung it at James, who ducked, laughing.

They hurled snowballs at each other until their fingers were numb inside their wet gloves, and then made their way to the post office. The store looked very festive, with tiny drifts of snow caught in the corner of each small windowpane. Mandy pushed open the door, stamping her feet to get rid of the snow sticking to her boots.

Mrs. McFarlane greeted them with a smile. "Come to see if the mail made it through?" she inquired. "It did — but only just. I hope we don't get much more snow. It would be such a shame if the Christmas mail didn't arrive."

"Is there a package here for my dad?" Mandy asked.

"I'll look for you, dear," said Mrs. McFarlane. "Just wait there a moment."

As she opened the door that led to the office, there was a fluttering sound. To Mandy's and James's astonishment, a blue parakeet flew out and landed on the post office counter with a friendly chirp.

"Oh!" Mrs. McFarlane came out of the office, looking flustered. "I thought I'd shut the cage, but it's all so new. . . . Oh, dear! Just a moment . . ."

From its perch on the counter, the little parakeet leaned its blue head to one side. It stared at Mandy, who stared back, enchanted. Mrs. McFarlane approached the bird rather gingerly, her hands extended. There was a pool of birdseed in her palm. The parakeet chirped again, then flew daintily to Mrs. McFarlane's hand and perched on her finger, its delicate claws spread out for balance.

"He was yesterday's special delivery," Mrs. McFarlane explained, closing her hand very gently over the bird's head and cupping her other hand around its body. "I've wanted a parakeet for ages, but there's an awful lot to learn about keeping them! Mr. McFarlane spent most of yesterday evening arranging the cage and toys but I think we may have to look at his cage's latch again — I'm sure I shut it. . . ." She began to carry the little bird back into the office.

"Oh, don't put him back in his cage yet," Mandy begged. "I'd like to meet him for real!"

Mrs. McFarlane slowly opened her hand. "I don't want him to fly off again," she said. "Everything must seem very new and strange to him."

"That's probably why he wants to explore," Mandy said. "Parakeets are very inquisitive birds." She reached out and stroked the bird's feathers very lightly. The waxy-looking ceres around his beak was blue, while his wings were speckled blue and white and his head was the color of a summer sky.

"What's his name?" James asked, reaching across to stroke the bird's head.

"We haven't had a chance to name him yet," Mrs. McFarlane admitted. "Maybe you and Mandy might like to help out?"

Mandy loved naming animals! "Bluey?" she suggested, looking at the gorgeous feathers on his head. "Or Speckle? Or how about Sky?"

James watched the parakeet picking his way through the bird food in Mrs. McFarlane's hand. The little bird seemed to be going for little yellow seeds before anything else. "He likes those seeds, doesn't he?"

"Those are sesame seeds," said Mrs. McFarlane. "I think the sunflower seeds are a little too big for him just yet."

"Sesame!" Mandy exclaimed. "That would be a great name!"

"Sesame?" echoed Mrs. McFarlane. "Yes, I like that. It has a sassy sort of sound that suits him. Thank you, Mandy. Sesame will do just fine."

"Sesame," Mandy repeated, feeling pleased as she watched the little bird crack another of his favorite seeds in his beak. "Perfect."

"Now," said Mrs. McFarlane, "I think Sesame should

go back in his cage. I'm going to be busy again today. With Walton Road being closed, everyone in Welford has to do their shopping here! Your father's package wasn't in the office, Mandy, dear. Maybe it will arrive tomorrow."

"Bye, Sesame," Mandy said softly as Mrs. McFarlane walked back to the office with Sesame cupped in her hand. "See you soon."

Mrs. McFarlane turned around. "I'll tell you what," she said. "We're putting up our Christmas tree this afternoon, and it's not as easy for me to put the decorations on the top branches as it used to be. Would you two like to come back and help me? You could play with Sesame again, if you'd like to."

"Yes, please!" Mandy and James said together.

Mrs. McFarlane laughed. "Four o'clock, then," she said. "See you later!"

Mandy felt like skipping all the way back to Animal Ark. The frost and snow looked so beautiful and sparkly, and her head was full of Sesame and his soft blue feathers. She loved decorating Christmas trees, too — it would be the icing on the cake for a fantastic day.

"Looks like the snow agrees with someone," remarked Jean Knox as Mandy came into the clinic.

"It's gorgeous out there," Mandy agreed. "And guess what? The McFarlanes got a parakeet! He's the cutest thing."

The waiting room was busy, with several patients and their owners occupying the chairs. Mandy recognized one of them immediately.

"Hi, Button!" she exclaimed, crouching down to stroke a dark brown rabbit in the lap of a dark-haired, serious-looking boy. "What's up with Button, John?" she asked.

John was Julian Hardy's son. He was away at boarding school during the school year, but came back to live with his father and stepmother at the Fox and Goose during the vacations. "Button's got a problem with her foot," he said. "She won't put her weight on it this morning."

Dr. Adam put his head around the consulting room door. "Bring Button on in, John," he said. "Ah, Mandy — could you come and give me a hand? Your mom got called out to Mrs. Forsyth's farm, and Simon managed to get himself snowed in, so we're a little short-staffed."

Dr. Adam examined Button's foot carefully while Mandy wriggled into the spare white coat that hung on the back of her dad's consulting room door. He asked Mandy to get some warm water and a bandage from the cupboard, then turned to John.

"One of Button's toes is a little frostnipped," he explained. "We need to warm it up before it gets worse."

"Frostbite?" John said anxiously. "Does that mean you'll have to amputate her toe?"

Mandy handed her dad a shallow bowl half-filled with warm water. Dr. Adam held Button's foot in the water and began expertly massaging the rabbit's toe. "It's not frostbite yet," he said, holding out his hand for a towel and then the bandage. "Button should be OK if we wrap that toe so it's close to the rest of her warm body. Keep her out of any drafts, and don't let her hop around in the snow."

Button wriggled in Dr. Adam's hands as he bound her foot so it pressed against her fluffy tummy. Mandy felt a pang for the unhappy rabbit. Maybe the snow wasn't *completely* great after all.

Two more patients were also suffering from the cold: a cat with runny eyes and a bad wheeze, and an arthritic German shepherd. Mandy thought about Tarka as she helped her dad lift the old dog onto the table, and wondered if Lauren had said anything to her mom about bringing the spaniel into the clinic.

The last patient was a parrot who had suffered a bad reaction to some fabric-cleaning spray.

"Between you and me, that could have been fatal,"

Dr. Adam told Mandy, as they washed their hands and prepared to go into the kitchen to grab some lunch. "If that parrot had been the size of a parakeet, it probably would have been. Birds can be extremely sensitive to toxic substances."

"Mrs. McFarlane's got a new parakeet." Mandy told her dad all about Sesame as they sat down at the kitchen table.

"Any sign of my package?" Dr. Adam asked.

"Not yet." Mandy covered a piece of bread with her grandmother's plum jam and spread a thick layer of peanut butter on the top piece of bread. Helping in the clinic always made her hungry. "She said to come in again tomorrow."

Dr. Adam put down the butter knife, looking worried. Before Mandy could ask him what the problem was, the door banged open and Dr. Emily came in.

"You've got to come and see what Mrs. Forsyth's given us," said Mandy's mom, breathless and pink-cheeked from the cold. "She wanted to say thank you for coming to her farm in the snow."

Mandy peered out of the door. A fat, bushy Christmas tree, still covered with a dusting of snow, lay on the back seat of the Land Rover, its topmost branches curled against the side window. Between the three of them, they managed to carry it inside, taking care not to knock any dishes off the kitchen table as they squeezed through the door and into the living room.

"Just as well we've already had the Christmas Dance Committee Meeting," Dr. Adam puffed. "This tree takes up half the house!"

"The stand is in the cabinet by the TV, Mandy," Dr. Emily directed from somewhere behind the tree's frosty green branches.

"This means I've got two Christmas trees to decorate today!" Mandy realized happily, pulling the tree stand out of the cabinet and putting it down in the corner.

Dr. Adam trimmed the base of the tree and settled it neatly in the stand. He gave its branches a gentle shake, and a light sprinkling of snow fell on the carpet. "Whose is the other tree?" he asked.

"Mrs. McFarlane's," Mandy explained. "She asked me and James to help because she can't reach the highest branches."

Dr. Emily checked her watch. "We've got to get back to work," she said regretfully, staring at the tree. "I guess we'll have to leave the decorating to you, Mandy. You know where the decorations are kept. See you later!"

"And go easy on the purple tinsel," Dr. Adam pleaded before following Mandy's mom out to the clinic.

Mandy ran to the cabinet under the stairs and pulled

out the box of Christmas decorations. Here was the rather dented-looking angel she'd made last year out of an egg box and some gold glitter; here was the box of glass star decorations her grandparents had brought back from Austria two years ago; here was all the glittery tinsel the Hopes had collected since Mandy was a baby. Last of all, Mandy pulled out the string of Christmas lights. That was the best part, she decided, as she carefully wound the lights around the tree — turning on the lights when it was dark outside. She'd save that for her parents after dinner tonight.

Dr. Adam popped his head around the living-room door. "Listen, Mandy, if you're seeing Mrs. McFarlane again this afternoon, just ask about my package again, will you? No hurry, it's just — well . . . Ask her, will you?"

"Sure," Mandy said, frowning as her dad disappeared back into the clinic.

What could be in the package that was making her dad so jumpy?

Five

Mandy finished decorating the tree by carefully fixing the angel to the top branch. The living room was beginning to darken. Thinking longingly of turning on the tree lights, Mandy stretched out her hand to the switch. But then she thought how much better it would be to see the full effect for the first time when her parents could see it, too. With a sigh, she pulled her hand away.

The phone rang.

"Remember about decorating Mrs. McFarlane's tree this afternoon!" said James.

"As if I'd forget!" Mandy smiled. "I've been practicing

on our own tree since lunchtime. Shall we head over there now?"

"See you there," said James. "Oh, and have you noticed? It's snowing again!"

Mandy looked out of the window. Sure enough, big fat flakes were rolling out of the sky, dusting the windowpanes. "I'll be at the post office in twenty minutes," she promised and hung up.

Wrapping herself in her longest, warmest scarf, Mandy set out into the darkening afternoon. The sun hung very low and orange on the horizon where the clouds had thinned, making the snow sparkle and gleam like powdered glass. *Wouldn't it be wonderful to catch that sparkle?* Mandy thought as she skated and twirled on the frozen puddles. *Catch it and frame it.*

"Come in, come in!" Mrs. McFarlane ushered Mandy and James out of the cold. "Bring Blackie, too, James. It's much too cold to leave him outside."

Mandy stared appreciatively at Mrs. McFarlane's beautiful Christmas tree. It was taller and more slender than the tree Mrs. Forsyth had given them, with plenty of space between the branches for lights and tinsel. Mr. McFarlane waved from behind the counter, where he was serving a long line of Christmas customers, and they waved back.

"How's Sesame, Mrs. McFarlane?" Mandy asked.

"Perky as ever," Mrs. McFarlane reported. She nodded at the birdcage, which she'd hung in a quiet corner of the store, not far from the Christmas tree. Sesame blinked at Mandy with bright beady eyes, and ruffled his wings. "I thought we could let him sit out here, so he sees a few more people. He seems to like all the hustle and bustle. Maybe we could let him out for some exercise after we've finished the tree."

James frowned at Blackie. "You can't chase Sesame," he said sternly. "If you do, I'll put you outside and you can turn into a snow dog."

Mandy grinned at the thought of Blackie looking like a dog-shaped snowman. She couldn't imagine him sitting still long enough to be covered from head to tail! Mrs. McFarlane had put several boxes of Christmas decorations at the foot of the tree. She opened the nearest box and lifted a delicate golden sleigh from its bed of tissue paper.

"I remember this one from when I was a girl," she murmured. "It catches the Christmas tree lights beautifully."

James and Mandy opened the rest of the boxes, uncovering fragile glass balls, crystal slippers, snowmen, icicles, bears, and strings of brightly colored beads and lights. Everything looked antique, heavy, and detailed, and very well looked after. Mandy thought guiltily about her dented eggbox angel, and promised herself she would wrap up their decorations more carefully this year.

"Ah." Mrs. McFarlane pounced on a large, wrapped decoration at the bottom of the box. "The star for the very top. This is my favorite decoration of all."

A beautiful golden star studded with snowflake-shaped crystals emerged from the sheets of tissue paper. Mandy picked it up very carefully. It was surprisingly heavy, made from a single piece of metal that had been beaten into the distinctive five-pointed shape.

"My grandmother used to tell me that this star had fallen out of the sky," Mrs. McFarlane said as Mandy and James admired it. "You can see why, can't you?"

Mandy could. It seemed very real somehow — twinkly, heavy, and with a burnished shine on it that made her think of the brass horses she had seen in an antique store in Walton.

"I'll go and find the stepladder," said Mrs. McFarlane, getting to her feet. "Those top branches will be tricky otherwise."

Aside from those in line for packages and letters, there were several customers in the aisles, picking up books and toys. *They must be mailing Christmas presents*, Mandy guessed. An uneasy thought returned to nag her. What was she going to give everyone for

Christmas, now that shopping in Walton was out of the question?

"What are you doing about Christmas presents, James?" she asked, twirling a tiny birdcage decoration in her fingers.

"Making them," said James. He hung a glass ball on one of the lower tree branches. "My dad's shed is full of parts and pieces of old stuff. I thought I'd put some of them together and see what I come up with."

"I'm not very good at building things," Mandy said gloomily. "What am I going to do?"

"You're pretty good at drawing and painting," James pointed out. "Why don't you do pictures for everyone? You could even put them in frames."

Mandy looked thoughtfully at Mrs. McFarlane's racks of paper and card stock. She had some paints. She could try to paint some snowy landscapes — there were plenty of views at home she could try. She probably wouldn't be able to capture that frosty sparkle, but . . .

Suddenly, an idea popped into her head. "You're brilliant, James!" she gasped, jumping to her feet.

"I am?" said James, looking confused. "Why?"

Mandy went over to the racks of white card stock and started riffling through them. "It's a secret," she said. "But you'll love it." Clutching a package of white card stock and a little hardback folder, she joined the line of customers. It would take a few days to paint everything, but she would still have time for the finishing touch — as long as the weather stayed nice and cold and snowy.

She paid for the card stock, tucked it into the folder, and brought it back to where James was still hanging decorations on the tree. Blackie lay with his head on his paws, watching.

"Here's the stepladder." Mrs. McFarlane came puffing over. "It took a little time to find it among all the Christmas packages we're trying to deal with at the moment."

Mandy suddenly remembered something. "Did my dad's package arrive in the second delivery today?"

"I'm afraid not, dear," said Mrs. McFarlane. "I looked out for it specially."

"Dad's getting a little jumpy about it," Mandy explained, helping Mrs. McFarlane to set up the ladder.

"I can believe it," Mrs. McFarlane said. "This snow is a terrible nuisance."

Mandy caught James's eye. Would grown-ups never stop complaining about the snow?

James had just set foot on the ladder when the doorbell tinkled, and Lauren came in with Tarka on a tartan leash. Although the spaniel was still walking awkwardly, her hindlegs seemed a little less stiff than before. She recognized Mandy right away, and pulled at her leash

until Lauren let her come over to say hello. Mandy
rubbed her feather-soft head, and the spaniel thumped
her heavy tail delightedly against the floor.

"Hi, there," said Lauren. "How are the dance plans?"

"It should be OK," said James. "As long as they open
Walton Road in time for the DJ to get here."

Mandy stared at James in dismay. She hadn't thought
of that. "What are we going to do if he can't?"

"My mom could come and play if you were really des-
perate," Lauren joked.

"Your mom's in a band, isn't she?" Mandy said, remembering. "What kind of music does she play?"

"Folk," said Lauren. "But it's kind of punky and fun,
not full of bearded old guys with harmonicas. Her band's
pretty well known actually, if you're into the folk scene."

"What's the band called?" James asked with interest.

"Cloud Dancers," said Lauren. "Listen, could you do
me a quick favor? I'm knitting my mom a Christmas
stocking and I need some more wool. When Mom comes
home, it won't be so easy to get the stocking finished
without her knowing. Mrs. McFarlane's got some great
colors, but that line looks kind of long. Do you mind
watching Tarka for me? She'll end up knocking stuff off
the shelves if she gets too close. You've seen how clumsy
she is."

Tarka licked happily at Mandy's hands as if she was

more than happy to stay with her. "Did you knit that sweater you were wearing the other day?" Mandy asked Lauren.

Lauren nodded, her cheeks going slightly pink. "Did you like it? It was my own design." She looked down at the chunky black-and-white cardigan she was wearing. "So's this."

"I'd love to be able to knit," Mandy said, admiring the striking cardigan. "Maybe I could knit a few Christmas presents."

"You won't have time," James warned her. "Knitting takes ages."

"You can learn basic skills pretty quickly," said Lauren. "I'll show you sometime if you like. I'm kind of busy right now looking after Tarka because Mom's away again, but maybe you could come over one afternoon?"

"Thanks, I'd love to!" Mandy said gratefully.

"Has your mom been snowed in somewhere?" James asked.

"No, she's back with Grandpa," Lauren said. "He's been sick lately, and she didn't want to leave him with all this snow." She glanced at Tarka with a sigh. "So guess who's looking after the dog again?"

"It's a shame it's too cold to take Tarka swimming," Mandy said, stroking Tarka's ears. "Swimming's really good for stiff joints."

Lauren looked surprised. "I don't think Tarka would fit in at the local swimming pool, do you?"

"Dogs don't swim in human pools," Mandy explained. "They can swim in lakes or rivers, or go to special hydrotherapy pools for animals. It's really good for them. Tarka's legs look a little better today, by the way."

"It's probably got something to do with sleeping on my bed," said Lauren wryly. "I keep having to kick her off my pillows. Thanks for watching Tarka. I'll be back in a minute."

She picked up three balls of wool from the display: a greeny-gold, a cherry-red, and a bright and zingy yellow. Then she joined the line of customers.

"If I had a gorgeous dog like you, Tarka, I would never kick you off my bed." Mandy sighed, dropping a kiss on the spaniel's warm head.

"Your mom might have something to say about that," James joked from the top of the stepladder, where he was carefully fixing the gold star into position.

Sesame chirped and fluttered in his cage, beating his wings against the bars.

"Sesame's getting restless," Mrs. McFarlane observed, coming over to see how Mandy and James were doing. "Maybe it's time to let him fly around a little."

She reached up to unhinge the cage door. To Mandy's delight, Sesame flew out of the door as if he couldn't

wait to explore, and perched on a rack of birthday cards with his head tilted to one side. Tarka pricked her ears and Blackie whined longingly as the tiny bird took off and zoomed to the other end of the store.

"He's adorable!" Mandy laughed as the parakeet zipped neatly through the Christmas decorations that hung accordion-style from the ceiling.

Sesame swooped in a full circle and landed on a branch of the Christmas tree just as the post office door opened with its customary jangle of bells. An icy draft swept around the store, making the streamers rustle. At once, Sesame launched himself toward the gap in the door.

"Oh, no, you don't!" Mandy launched herself at him — but as she stretched out her hand to shut the door, all the lights went out.

Six

The post office was blanketed in darkness. In the first moment of stunned silence, Tarka pressed her warm, solid body against Mandy's knees and whined.

"It's OK, Tarka," Mandy soothed, feeling the top of Tarka's head and stroking her ears very gently. Her other hand banged into the bottom of the stepladder.

"Hey!" said James, from somewhere above her. "Watch out!"

Mandy peered up at his shadowy outline. "Be careful," she said anxiously.

"I'm OK," said James, gingerly climbing down the ladder, feeling each rung with his toes. "What happened?"

Gradually, their eyes became accustomed to the dark. Mandy could see through the window that all the other lights in Welford seemed to have gone out as well.

"It must be a blackout!" Mrs. McFarlane tutted in annoyance. "What a nuisance. And where has Sesame gone? He's hard enough to see with all the lights on!"

Mandy's hand flew to her mouth. "The door!" she gasped. "I was trying to shut it when the lights went out. Do you think he might have gotten outside?"

It was hard to see Mrs. McFarlane's expression in the dark. When she spoke, her voice sounded strained. "I suppose he might have. Was he very close to the door?"

"Yes," said Mandy, feeling wretched.

A flashlight beam suddenly swept around the room and coats rustled as people put up their arms to shield their eyes.

"Sorry, everyone," Mr. McFarlane apologized, waving the flashlight. "We'll have to close for the rest of the day. The cash register's not working, and I can't see much back here."

A few customers muttered with annoyance, but everyone could see that Mr. McFarlane was right. Reluctantly, they started moving toward the door.

"One at a time, please." Mrs. McFarlane held the door open just enough for the customers to leave the post office in single file. "We have a parakeet on the loose. One at a time, please . . . So sorry . . ."

"I think I was the last one Mr. McFarlane served," Lauren said, looking relieved as she tucked her wool into her shoulder bag. "I would never have been able to get Mom's stocking finished if I hadn't bought the wool today." She took Tarka's leash from Mandy. "Did Mrs. McFarlane say her bird had gotten loose?"

Mandy was extremely worried. "He might have flown out the door," she said. "He's very small, and Mrs. McFarlane's only had him for a couple of days. If he's outside, he might not find his way home again."

Mrs. McFarlane shut the door behind the last customer. Everyone looked up at the ceiling.

"We should split up and look for him," James suggested. "Blackie and I can look outside."

"I'll stay and help," Lauren offered.

Mandy and Lauren helped the McFarlanes to hunt around the post office with the help of Mr. McFarlane's flashlight. Lauren shushed Tarka, who was whining with excitement, as they listened carefully for the fluttering of tiny bird wings.

Mandy heard something first. Full of relief, she pointed at the Christmas tree. "Over there, Mr. McFarlane!"

"Where?" Mr. McFarlane shone the beam among the

bushy, top branches of the Christmas tree. Mandy could see a silver bear, and a straw gingerbread man, and a little blue bird-shaped ornament. . . .

The ornament ruffled his wings and chirped.

"Sesame!" Mandy cried. "I thought you were one of the decorations!" She put her foot on the bottom rung of the stepladder.

"What if he flies off again?" Mrs. McFarlane asked anxiously.

"I think it'll be all right." Mandy climbed a little farther up the ladder. "When it gets dark, birds think it's bedtime and they usually try and go to sleep. I bet that's what Sesame's doing."

Lauren held on to the bottom of the ladder as Mandy reached up for the little bird. Sesame blinked sleepily at Mandy as she lifted him down.

"Back into your cage, little fellow," she said gently, climbing down the ladder. She felt Sesame's claws scratch her skin like tiny pins as he clung on.

Mr. McFarlane lit some candles while Mrs. McFarlane lifted down the birdcage. At last, Sesame was returned safely to his perch and the cage door was firmly shut.

The door tinkled. "No sign of Sesame outside," James reported, stamping his feet on the mat and shutting the door as quickly as he could. "Sorry. I looked and looked —"

"It's OK," Mandy said. "We found him." She nodded at Mrs. McFarlane, who had put her face to the bars of the cage and was making soothing noises at the little parakeet.

"I've gotta go." Lauren hitched up her shoulder bag and twitched Tarka's leash. "Come on, dog. I've got a lot of knitting to do before Mom comes home."

"Bye, Lauren. Bye, Tarka." Mandy watched as Tarka limped out of the post office door. Even though the spaniel seemed more comfortable today, that didn't mean she couldn't have something wrong with her hips. Mandy decided she would talk to Lauren's mom about Tarka as soon as she could.

The silhouette of Mr. Gill, a local pig farmer, appeared at the door. "Any chance of getting a few stamps, Mrs. McFarlane?" he asked, peering through the gloom.

"Sorry, Mr. Gill, not this afternoon," said Mrs. McFarlane.

Mr. Gill took off his woolen hat and scratched his head. "What a nuisance," he said. "Apparently the snow's brought down a power line between Welford and Walton."

"So all of Welford's blacked out?" Mandy asked in dismay.

"Blacked out and cut off, too," said Mr. Gill. "Walton Road's still closed. I'll drop by tomorrow and see if you can manage a couple of stamps for me then, Mrs. McFarlane. My Christmas cards are really late."

"Thank you for all your help, you two," Mrs. McFarlane said, as Mandy and James followed Mr. Gill out of the post office. "It's such a relief that Sesame's safe. And the tree looks lovely, too," she added.

"Looks like we'll have to do without the Christmas lights, though," Mr. McFarlane joked before he shut the door behind them.

"Our Christmas tree lights!" Mandy groaned. "I wanted to turn them on tonight."

"If this blackout lasts until Christmas Day, we won't have any lights on the Christmas tree outside the Fox and Goose, either," James said thoughtfully as they walked along the darkened road. "The village will look really boring without them, even though we've got the snow."

Mandy didn't reply. Her lips were starting to tingle in the icy wind, and her toes had already gone numb inside her boots. No Christmas presents, no tree lights, no packages . . . Suddenly, she wished the snow would go away.

Back in the Hopes' kitchen, candles were flickering merrily on every surface. Mandy started to feel a little more cheerful as she unwound her scarf. The house looked really twinkly and Christmassy, even without the tree lights. All she needed now was a hot bowl of tomato soup to wrap her chilly fingers around.

"Cold lasagna and bread for supper, I'm afraid." Mandy's mom put out plates, along with butter and grated parmesan.

"Nothing hot at all?" asked Mandy in dismay.

"Afraid not, with the blackout." Dr. Emily sliced the bread.

"I was going to look for the old camp stove in the attic, but the clinic has been so busy that I never made it," said Dr. Adam, helping himself to a slice of lasagna. "I'll find it tomorrow before we really start to get hungry!"

"I don't know how we're going to manage if the power is still off." Dr. Emily sighed. "Lots of our equipment, including the clinic phone, the photocopier, and the computer, will be useless. Thank goodness our cell phones are fully charged."

Mandy put down her bread. "Do you think the power will be off for a while?" she asked.

Dr. Emily shrugged. "With Walton Road closed, all of Welford's snowed in, Mandy. No one's going to get through to fix that power line tonight."

In the living room, Dr. Adam lit a fire, which crackled and leaped in the grate. As there was no television,

Mandy got out an old pack of cards and they played a few rounds of Crazy Eights. Dr. Emily managed to heat up enough water in a saucepan over the fire for three hot-water bottles.

Later that evening, with a hot-water bottle tucked inside her sweater, Mandy sat in her bedroom and carefully began her Christmas gift project by the light of a flickering candle. She had a few ideas that would be perfect for her parents and her grandparents. She tried to come up with something just as good for James, but that was trickier. She frowned. If she couldn't do a picture for James, what was she going to do?

When Dr. Emily put her head around the door, Mandy quickly put her arm over what she was doing.

"What are you up to?" her mother asked. "Is that a picture?"

"You'll find out on Christmas Day," Mandy said, being deliberately mysterious.

Her mom held up her hands and smiled. "I get the message. I promise I won't ask again. Sleep well, Mandy. See you in the morning."

The light in Mandy's room the following morning was the same eerie bright white of the day before. Mandy flicked her bedside lamp to check if the power had returned, but the bulb remained stubbornly dark. She rolled over and stared out the window at the snow-covered fields. It still looked gorgeous, but suddenly the problems the snow had brought seemed easier to remember than its beauty.

After sloshing her face with cold water and brushing her teeth, Mandy headed downstairs for breakfast. The welcome smell of oatmeal met her as she came into the kitchen.

"Hot breakfast!" Mandy leaned forward and sniffed eagerly at the oatmeal pot in the center of the table. "How did you do it, Mom?"

Dr. Emily pointed at an ancient camping stove attached to a squat blue gas bottle that sat on the kitchen counter. "Your dad brought it down from the attic this morning," she said.

"I wish we could power up the clinic's computer on gas," said Dr. Adam, sipping his coffee. "Thank goodness Jean's the kind of receptionist who keeps everything written down on paper."

"You don't have to do any operations today, do you?" Mandy asked anxiously. She hated the thought of sick animals having to wait for treatment because of the lack of electricity.

"Nothing on the books," said Dr. Adam. "Let's hope we don't have any emergencies."

Scraping up the last spoonful of oatmeal, Mandy

thought of Tarka. She hoped that the lovely dog hadn't slept out in Lauren's hallway last night. Weather like this would only make her hips worse.

"I'm going into the village to see if Lauren's mom is at home, to talk to her about Tarka," she told her parents as they cleared away the breakfast things. "I'll go and see the McFarlanes again, too. Sesame nearly escaped last night, and I want to see how he is. Oh, and while I'm there I could check for your package again, Dad."

Dr. Adam was scrubbing hard at the oatmeal saucepan. "Don't worry about it, Mandy," he said.

"But you said it was important," Mandy reminded him.

"I don't think Bill will make it through all this snow," said Dr. Emily. Bill Ward was the Welford postman.

"That's sad." Mandy sighed. "Think of all those Christmas presents and cards that won't arrive in time."

Once the table was cleared, she put on her thickest parka and crunched out in the snow. The sky was much bluer today, as if the snow had finished falling for a little while. She kicked away the powdery covering of snow over the iced-up puddles as she walked into the village, and admired the frosty ivy leaves cascading down the hedgerows.

She met James and Blackie coming the other way. Mandy laughed when she saw a tiny triangle of snow on the tip of Blackie's nose. It looked like James's Labrador had been digging in the snowdrifts.

"What do you want to do today?" James asked.

Stroking an enthusiastic Blackie, Mandy told him about her plans to visit Sesame and Lauren's mom. "You don't know if the mail has arrived today, do you?" she asked.

"If it has, then Bill's got a big job delivering it," James said, as they reached the Welford crossroads.

Just then, Blackie pricked up his ears and barked. Mandy stopped and turned to see a very unexpected vehicle come bumping around the corner toward them.

"Morning!" called Bill Ward cheerfully. He let go of the handlebars of the four-wheeled all-terrain vehicle and waved to them. The sleek dark blue body of the machine was dwarfed by its huge black wheels, which rolled confidently over the snow, and a small two-wheeled trailer was hitched behind it. Bill's black-and-tan Australian cattle dog, Tara, stood beside him, her tongue lolling out and her breath misting in the air.

"What do you think of my new mail van?" Bill asked as he pulled alongside them.

"It's an ATV!" Mandy gasped. "And a trailer, too! That's such a good idea!"

Bill Ward shrugged modestly. "I borrowed them from

Ken Hudson yesterday," he said. "It was the only way to get to the sorting facility in Walton this morning. I couldn't let the Christmas mail go undelivered, could I?"

James was peering in the back of the trailer. "Come and see all these bags of letters and packages, Mandy!" he called. "It's like Christmas!"

He stopped as Mandy and Bill both roared with laughter.

"Well, it *is* Christmas," Mandy pointed out between giggles.

"Hop in if you'd like a lift into the village," Bill suggested. "I've got to go back to the post office for something. I can only go about two miles an hour on this thing, so you'll be quite safe."

"Perfect," said Mandy, jumping on the back of the trailer. "We were going to the post office, anyway."

She gave James a hand into the trailer. Blackie jumped up as well, and sniffed at Tara in a friendly manner. Bill started up the quad-bike and they set off with only the tiniest jerk.

"How are Delilah and Daisy?" Mandy shouted at Bill, raising her voice over the roar of the engine. Delilah and Daisy were Bill's two white Persian cats.

"I thought I'd lost them yesterday afternoon," Bill called back over his shoulder. "It's pretty hard finding white cats in the snow. I was out looking for them when I saw two pairs of green eyes floating toward me. It gave me quite a scare, I can tell you."

The ATV drove on, squashing the drifting snow beneath its enormous wheels. Mandy waved at the people who had stopped to stare at their strange procession. "I feel like I'm in a carnival!" she said.

She wriggled to get more comfortable. Something hard was digging into her — a large, lumpy-looking package.

She laughed out loud when she read the address.

"This must be the package Dad's been waiting for," she told James. She gave it a careful shake.

"It might be fragile," James said. "Stop shaking it, Mandy. Your dad will be mad if you break it."

The McFarlanes were very pleased with Bill Ward's unusual delivery of two- and four-legged packages! When Mandy asked to see Sesame, Mrs. McFarlane motioned her over to the cage, which now hung just behind the post office counter. "We thought we'd keep him back here for a couple of days," she said. "He's taking a little while to recover from his adventure last night."

Sesame was sitting hunched up on his perch. As Mandy watched, he seemed to totter sideways, then haul himself upright again. His feathers were fluffed up as if he'd been standing in a strong breeze.

"Poor Sesame," Mandy said. "He looks like he needs to catch up on his rest. Oh, and I've got Dad's package, so you don't need to look out for it anymore, Mrs. McFarlane."

Mandy and James left the post office and walked together toward Lauren's house. As they reached the edge of the village, Mandy spotted Lauren and Tarka in the field. Vaulting over the stile at the end of the road, she waded through the pristine snow to greet them.

"Hi, there," said Lauren through chattering teeth. "I'm

freezing out here, but Mom insisted that I take Tarka for a walk this morning. Oh, stop jumping around for just one second, will you?" she snapped at Tarka as the spaniel lay on her back, squirming at Mandy's feet. "I'm *trying* to have a conversation!"

"I love your scarf," Mandy told Lauren, trying to lighten the older girl's mood. "Did you knit it yourself?"

Lauren twirled the end of her long pink-and-cream scarf. "Yes, I made it last Christmas," she said. "Knitting is so relaxing. You're going to love it. Are you still up for that lesson?"

"You bet!" said Mandy.

Behind them, James had unfastened Blackie's leash to let him stretch his legs. The Labrador bounded over to Tarka with a playful bark. Tarka tried to jump up and kiss Blackie on the nose, but she toppled over in the snow instead.

"Tarka looks stiffer today," Mandy commented.

"Mom says this weather's really hard on her joints," Lauren said as Tarka scrambled slowly to her feet. "She insisted that Tarka sleep by the fire last night, not in the hallway. I wouldn't have minded sleeping there myself. My bedroom was freezing!"

Blackie dug his nose in the snow, then threw his head up and began chasing Tarka across the field. The spaniel barked happily and tried to run away.

"Careful!" Mandy called. But the two dogs kept running toward the stone wall at the edge of the field.

"It's OK," said Lauren. "Tarka could use the exercise. She's getting pretty fat in her old age."

Blackie took a flying leap at the wall and vanished over the other side. Mandy watched in horror as Tarka tried to follow. Her front paws made it to the top of the wall, but her hind legs didn't have enough spring in them to push her all the way. With her front feet scrambling helplessly on the icy stones, she lost her balance and tumbled backward off the wall, landing on the snow-packed ground with a dreadful *crunch*.

Seven

Mandy rushed over to where Tarka was lying in the snow, trying to get up. Her hind leg hung behind her, looking limp and useless. Mandy's heart was in her mouth as she knelt beside the injured dog and felt along the leg bone. The old dog gave a shrill yelp of pain.

"Is she OK?" Lauren demanded, kneeling beside Mandy.

"I think she's broken her leg," Mandy said, trying to stop her voice from trembling. "We shouldn't really move her without a splint, but she can't stay out here in the snow."

Lauren unwrapped her scarf, and Mandy tied it around

Tarka's injured back leg to act as a temporary support for the broken bone. James took off his coat and put it carefully around the shivering dog. Blackie ran around in circles, sniffing anxiously at Tarka.

Lauren helped Mandy carry Tarka to the stile. As they hoisted the dog over, Tarka blinked at them with pain-filled, beseeching eyes. "We need to get Tarka to Animal Ark," Mandy said. "Oh, this snow!"

Lauren called her mom on her cell phone and explained what had happened. Then Lauren and James took turns helping Mandy carry the injured spaniel, taking care not to bump her injured leg. It was a long, slow walk through freezing drifts — and with every step, Mandy wished the snow would disappear. She wanted to hold Tarka tightly and tell her the pain would go away, but she didn't dare touch the spaniel's leg in case she caused more damage to the broken bone. *It's my fault*, she thought desperately as they trudged along. *I should have stopped her when she ran off with Blackie.*

At last, they reached the clinic, where Mandy's parents were about to take a break. Dr. Adam took one look at Tarka and ushered them into a consulting room. He felt Tarka's leg with gentle fingers as Mandy explained what happened.

"It was my fault," Mandy said. "I knew there was

something wrong with her hind legs, and I shouldn't have let her try to jump the wall."

"No, it was Blackie's fault," said James miserably.

"It was nobody's fault," said Dr. Adam. "Accidents happen all the time. Right now, we need to set this bone as quickly as we can. It's a nasty break, and she's torn the skin on her hock as well."

After sedating Tarka, Dr. Adam worked swiftly to stitch the wound and wrap the leg in a bandage made of special plastic, that would set fast and keep the bones in place. Lauren, Mandy, and James waited anxiously. It wasn't easy. The consulting room had just one window, and Mandy was acutely aware of how difficult it was to set a broken leg without good light. Numbly, she stroked Tarka's ears as her dad finished the bandage.

"That's the best I can do in the circumstances," Dr. Adam said, straightening up and rubbing the back of his neck. "Now we just have to make sure she gets plenty of rest." He glanced at Mandy. "I can see why you thought Tarka might be in the early stages of hip dysplasia. Her back legs don't sit properly in their sockets, do they?"

Lauren looked puzzled. "Hipdis — what?"

Mandy's dad explained. "It's a genetic trait, quite common in spaniels," he said, washing his hands and drying them on a towel hanging by the door. "The hip joints erode so that the leg bones don't fit into the sockets anymore. The hips are literally "displaced." It's manageable if treated, although unfortunately it's not curable. If it goes untreated, an animal can become very lame, and ultimately won't be able to walk at all. There are new breeding restrictions these days, particularly for bigger dogs who suffer from it the most, so the condition is being passed on less and less. But it's a difficult one to diagnose as it shares so many symptoms with other joint problems. I'd need to take an X-ray to be sure."

Lauren glanced around the dark consulting room. "And you need electricity for that, right?" she said.

Dr. Adam nodded. "It's a nasty condition, but it's not the end of the world," he said gently. "And of course, that leg needs to heal first," he pointed out. "In the meantime, as a precaution, make sure Tarka sleeps somewhere that's free of drafts. I'll prescribe some dietary supplements — we can start with glucosamine to lubricate the joints and keep them working smoothly. And I'll give you a gentle regimen of exercises for her."

Mandy noticed that Tarka was waking up and trying to struggle into a standing position. She bent down and stroked her, gazing into the spaniel's trusting brown eyes. "The pain's gone now, Tarka," she murmured. "You're going to be OK."

"Careful!" Dr. Adam picked up the spaniel and set her on the floor. They all watched as Tarka took a few tentative steps in her new plaster cast.

"I'll make sure that Tarka takes her supplements," Lauren said flatly. "Can I pick them up from the receptionist?"

Mandy glanced at her. What was Lauren thinking? She had really hoped that at last Lauren had realized that Tarka was a special dog who needed special care.

As they came out of the consulting room, Mandy remembered her dad's package. She pulled it out of her bag. "Pretty heavy supplies, Dad," she joked, passing it over.

Before Dr. Adam could say anything, a tall, dark-haired woman in a flamboyant red-and-yellow printed velvet scarf rushed through the door of the clinic and hurried over. "I got here as quickly as I could," she said, giving Lauren a kiss and bending down to stroke Tarka's silky head. "Is everything OK?"

"This is my mom, Vanessa Morley." Lauren introduced them all as Tarka sat on the floor, still looking dazed.

Vanessa Morley gave a strained-looking smile. "Please, call me Vanessa," she said, shaking Dr. Adam's hand. "I'm sorry we've had to meet under these circumstances. Thank you so much for your help with Tarka."

"I've explained to Lauren that Tarka may be in the early stages of hip dysplasia," Dr. Adam told Vanessa. "Tarka needs a warm place to sleep, and only the gentlest of exercise until she's well enough for an X-ray to confirm our suspicions."

"You poor old thing!" Vanessa exclaimed, scratching Tarka between the shoulder blades. "We'll have to take really good care of you."

Mandy was still watching Lauren. She hadn't approached Tarka at all, and looked like she'd rather be anywhere but at Animal Ark. Mandy wanted to tell her that everything would be OK, that hip dysplasia was a manageable problem with the right care. But she wasn't sure that Lauren was ready to listen just yet.

"Oh, I almost forgot." Vanessa straightened up again. "I came here via the post office, and there was a message from Mrs. McFarlane for you, Dr. Hope. She apologizes for not calling, but their phones are down, and they're snowed in there with all the last-minute Christmas business. Apparently their parakeet isn't well, and Mrs. McFarlane doesn't know what to do. She'd really appreciate it if you could go over there sometime today."

Mandy gasped. "Sesame's sick? But I just saw him this morning!" She suddenly remembered how quiet the little bird had been.

Dr. Emily emerged from the kitchen, a mug of coffee in her hand, and looked inquiringly at them all. Dr. Adam introduced Lauren and Vanessa, and Vanessa repeated Mrs. McFarlane's message.

"Did Mrs. McFarlane say what was the matter?" asked Dr. Emily, setting her coffee down on the reception desk.

Vanessa shook her head. "She did seem very worried, though," she said.

As Lauren and Vanessa left with Tarka limping between them, Mandy swung around to her mother. "Mom, we have to go over to the post office right away!" Her stomach was churning with guilt. *I should have noticed that Sesame wasn't well this morning*, she thought.

"I agree," said Dr. Emily. She glanced at Jean Knox. "How are the appointments looking, Jean?"

Jean Knox ran her finger down the page of the ledger. "Your next patient is at two o'clock."

"Will you be OK here without me, Adam?" Mandy's mom was already reaching for her overcoat and vet's bag.

"Jean and I will hold the fort down," Dr. Adam promised. "And Simon managed to call this morning on the cell phone. Apparently, the road is a little clearer, and he should make it into the clinic by lunchtime. Good luck with Sesame."

Mandy almost pulled her mother out of the clinic

door as James ran to untie Blackie. "Sesame was acting strangely this morning," she said, towing Dr. Emily along the snowy lane toward the village. "James noticed it, too, didn't you, James?"

"He looked pretty sorry for himself," James agreed.

"Birds tend to hide their illness until they are very sick," said Dr. Emily, skirting the icy puddles with long strides. "It's a survival thing, about not letting predators know when they are easy prey. That means it's very bad when they start to look unwell."

"I should have guessed there was a problem," Mandy berated herself. "But Mrs. McFarlane seemed to think he was just recovering from his adventure in the dark last night."

Dr. Emily took Mandy's hand as they approached the village crossroads. "It's not your fault, sweetie," she said. "You may know a great deal about animals, but you can't always second-guess a problem. Come on."

Mrs. McFarlane ran out from behind the counter as Mandy, James, and Dr. Emily entered the post office. "I'm so glad you're here," she said, motioning them toward the office door. "Sesame's not well at all. He's been lurching around like he's dizzy, and now he's sitting on the floor of his cage with his feathers fluffed up."

The windowless office was dimly lit with candles. Sesame's cage was standing on the table used for sorting the local mail. Through the narrow bars of the cage, Mandy could see Sesame squatting on the newspaper beneath his perch, his wings hunched miserably. Dr. Emily reached in and lifted him carefully out of the cage.

"Bring him through to the kitchen," said Mrs. McFarlane. "There's more light in there."

A strong shaft of sunshine was pouring in through the McFarlanes' kitchen window and illuminating the kitchen table. Dr. Emily set Sesame down on the festive red-and-green tablecloth, then opened her bag and began a careful examination of the little bird. Mandy watched as her mother unfurled Sesame's wings, studied his eyes and his beak, and shone a tiny light into his eyes.

"Has Sesame eaten anything unusual today?" Dr. Emily asked, looking up at Mrs. McFarlane who was hovering anxiously by her shoulder.

Mrs. McFarlane shook her head. "He hasn't eaten anything since last night," she said. "And that was just his usual food."

Dr. Emily pried open Sesame's beak and took a look down his throat. "Did you notice whether he'd ingested an unusual amount of grit to help with his digestion yesterday evening?"

"I don't put much grit in his cage," said Mrs. McFarlane. "Is that right?"

"Absolutely right." Dr. Emily nodded. "When small birds are sick, they can swallow a large quantity of grit in an attempt to make themselves feel better. It tends to makes things worse, actually. So we don't have to worry about that with young Sesame." She ran her finger down Sesame's shiny feathers. "Did his cage come from a reputable source?"

Mrs. McFarlane looked confused. "We got the cage that the breeder recommended," she said.

"Good." Mrs. Hope put Sesame down on the table again. "Unregulated cages are sometimes made from metals that are highly toxic to birds if they peck at the bars."

"Do you think he's been poisoned?" James gasped, his eyes very round behind his glasses.

"I can't tell without taking him back to Animal Ark for a thorough investigation," said Dr. Emily, "but it's possible. Birds have very delicate digestive systems, which are easily upset when they eat the wrong things. Another possibility is that he might have had some kind of dormant infection when you bought him, Mrs. McFarlane. These things sometimes take a few days to come out. Think hard about whether he's eaten anything unusual, will you? I think we should take Sesame back to the clinic and put him under observation. An X-ray might help, but this blackout means that's out of the question. We'll monitor him overnight, and let you know if we have a clearer diagnosis for you in the morning."

The post office Christmas decorations rustled overhead as Mandy pulled open the door. The noise reminded her of the flutter of Sesame's wings as he had flown around the store last night. It already seemed like a very long time ago.

Back at Animal Ark, Mandy, James, and Dr. Emily settled Sesame in a clean cage in the residential unit. James got some drinking water, and Mandy filled a bowl with food, including his favorite sesame seeds, to tempt him. But Sesame was still looking very poorly, hunched and quiet in the corner of the cage.

"Now all we can do is watch," said Dr. Emily, closing the cage door.

It doesn't seem like enough, Mandy thought desperately. *If only we could find out if he'd eaten something that was bad for him.* She trailed her fingers over the bars of Sesame's cage with a sigh. It wasn't the first time she wished she could talk to animals.

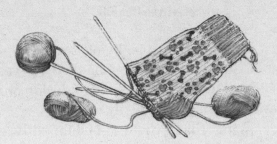

Eight

The following morning, there was still no power. As soon as she had dressed, Mandy crept down to the darkened residential unit to check on Sesame.

She found the little bird sitting exactly where they had left him the day before. Mandy put her face to the bars.

"You have to fight this, Sesame," she instructed the little bird. "It's Christmas in three days. You don't want to miss that, do you?"

Sesame seemed to hunch farther in on himself. With a heavy heart, Mandy left the residential unit and went to find her parents.

To her surprise, they weren't in the kitchen. She could

smell toast coming from the living room, so she followed her nose. Dr. Emily had banked up yesterday evening's fire so that it had been smoldering quietly all night. Now it was blazing merrily again.

"We're making toast the old-fashioned way," Dr. Emily announced, handing Mandy a fork and a piece of bread. "Hold it up to the fire and toast it like this." She demonstrated.

"I've been in to see Sesame," said Mandy, taking the fork and the bread and copying her mother. "I think he looks worse than yesterday."

Dr. Emily looked sad. "I know," she said. "We have to find out what's wrong with him as soon as possible."

"You still can't do an X-ray, can you?" Mandy said. "When's the electricity coming back on?"

"Jean says that her son knows someone who works for the power company," said Dr. Emily. "Even they can't say for sure until the snow melts enough to let the engineers through."

"Yesterday's sunshine must have helped," said Dr. Adam, buttering his toast and biting into it. "You know," he said after a moment, "this tastes different from the toast you get from the toaster. I wonder why?"

"Probably because it's got wood smoke all over it," Dr. Emily said, turning her fork around to toast the other side. "Mandy, are you going into the village today?"

Mandy nodded.

"We've got a busy day today," said Dr. Emily, "so we may not be able to stop in to see Mrs. McFarlane. Could you talk to her and see if she's come up with any more ideas about what Sesame might have eaten?"

Mandy washed the plates and swept up the toast crumbs in the living room. Then, once her parents had disappeared into the clinic to begin the day's work, she took out her scarf and hat and set out for the village. It was a bright, sunny day again and the surface of the snow had taken on a slightly watery sheen, but the wind was still bitingly cold.

"How is Sesame?" Mrs. McFarlane asked as soon as Mandy entered the post office.

"Not very well, I'm afraid." Mandy unwound her scarf.

"Mr. McFarlane and I thought and thought about what he could have eaten," said Mrs. McFarlane, "but we couldn't come up with a single thing. We've looked at everything on the shelves, in case Sesame left a nibble mark of some kind on one of the packages — laundry powder and that kind of thing, because I'm sure that can't be good for birds. But everything looked fine. I thought of calling the person we bought Sesame from, to check your mother's theory about an infection. But of course, the phone isn't working, so we drew a blank there as well. I simply don't know what else to do."

Mandy looked around the post office ceiling. The ceiling tiles looked unnibbled — so did the tinsel decorations that draped the room from corner to corner. The paint on the post office door was fresh and clean-looking. There wasn't a single clue to Sesame's illness to be seen.

Maybe it was an infection Sesame brought with him, after all, Mandy thought, as she said good-bye to Mrs. McFarlane and walked on to James's house. But that could be absolutely anything. They couldn't go on guessing forever. And she knew that Sesame was running out of time.

"I'm glad you came over," said James when he opened the door. "Blackie's feet are very sore from all that walking we did yesterday, and my toes practically froze off. I need some thicker socks for this weather, I'm wearing two ordinary pairs on top of each other." He held up his foot to demonstrate. Mandy could see a red sock peeping through the holey blue one on top.

Blackie looked up from his bed and thumped his tail in greeting as Mandy came into the kitchen.

"Sesame's still not well," Mandy reported as she bent down to stroke the black Labrador. "He hasn't moved since we put him in the residential unit yesterday. I wish he'd flutter his wings or something, but it's like he's giving up. I need something to cheer me up. How about going over to visit Tarka and Lauren?"

Blackie looked quite relieved to be left behind as James took down his coat and followed Mandy out into the snow. The sun gleamed on the trees and hills, dazzling Mandy's eyes so much that she had to shield her face as they trudged along Main Street to the Morleys' house.

Lauren seemed pleased to see them when she opened the door.

"Is your mom home?" Mandy asked as she hung up her coat.

Lauren shook her head. "She's back with Grandpa," she said. "This weather's a real problem for his chest, and the blackout isn't helping. Do you want to see Tarka?"

"How's she doing?" Mandy followed Lauren into the kitchen, with James close behind.

Lauren shrugged. "Well, she looks all right to me."

Tarka wriggled and whined happily when she saw Mandy and James. She tried to get up from her cozy spot beside the kitchen range, but she was still moving clumsily with her cast.

"You brave old thing." Mandy ruffled the spaniel's ears.

"Do you want something to drink?" Lauren offered. Mandy noticed that she hadn't even glanced at Tarka.

"You can have hot chocolate if you like. The range has oil burners, so we can heat milk there."

"That would be really nice, thanks," said Mandy. James nodded, too.

Lauren's project was sitting on the kitchen table, next to an old-fashioned oil lamp that cast a soft yellow glow over the miniature stage. Once she had put a pan of milk on the stove, Lauren sat down with her back to Tarka and picked up a little cluster of paper clips, which she was threading with clear glass beads.

James peered over Lauren's shoulder. "What are you making now?"

"A chandelier." Lauren swung the paper-clip creation between her fingertips. "If you wanted to do this full-scale, you could use wire coat-hangers and beads, or even Christmas ornaments. Do you like it?"

"It's beautiful," said James.

Mandy sat down next to Lauren and peered inside the theater set. She noticed that Lauren had added a few more dangling snowflakes to the Snow Queen's palace ceiling. "Did you finish your mom's Christmas stocking?" she asked.

Lauren nodded her head at a heap of brightly colored wool that was lying at the far end of the table. "Not quite," she said.

"Can I have a look, please?" When Lauren nodded,

Mandy stretched out her hand and picked up the huge, half-finished stocking. "It's covered in dog motifs!" she gasped, admiring the little bones and paw prints that Lauren had cleverly knitted into the pattern. Her heart leaped. Maybe Lauren was having a change of heart about Tarka after all.

"Mom's crazy about her dog," Lauren said shortly. "So I thought she'd go for a dog theme."

Feeling disappointed, Mandy pushed away from the table and went to help James pour out three cups of cocoa. Tarka sat up and pushed hopefully at Mandy's hand. As Mandy bent down to give the spaniel a good scratch between the shoulder blades, an odd, sweet smell wafted up to her. Mandy crouched down to take a closer look at the injured leg, and her heart sank. There were telltale stains around Tarka's cast that suggested a problem with the wound underneath. She kneeled down beside the Tarka and sniffed at her leg while the spaniel tried to lick Mandy's face. It definitely smelled bad. Then she felt Tarka's nose. It felt hot and rough. Mandy knew that this meant the dog was fighting a temperature.

She looked up at Lauren. "I think Tarka's got an infection underneath her cast," she said.

To her surprise, Lauren scowled. "Typical," she said. "Just typical."

"It's not her fault, Lauren," Mandy began.

"I know that," Lauren said. "It's just . . ." She stared at the paper clip chandelier in her hand, then suddenly threw it down. The tiny ornament bounced off the table with a clatter and landed on the floor.

Mandy looked at James, who raised his eyebrows as if to say, *Don't ask me what's going on.* Feeling very awkward, Mandy picked up the chandelier and put it on the table.

"I'm sorry, Lauren," she said, "but you'll have to bring Tarka back into the clinic."

"No, *I'm* sorry." Lauren ran her hand through her hair and really looked at Tarka for the first time since Mandy and James had arrived. "OK, what's wrong with her now?" she asked.

"Her leg doesn't smell right." Mandy gained confidence as she recognized a look of genuine concern on Lauren's face. "That's how you can tell whether an infection has set in."

"Gross," Lauren muttered. She sank to the ground and studied Tarka's cast. Tarka panted at her as she wrinkled her nose. "I see what you mean," she said, straightening up again. "Should I bring her to see your parents right now?"

"If that's OK," said Mandy. She thought of Lauren's college work waiting to be finished, and wondered what Lauren would say about this new interruption.

"Sure it's OK," said Lauren after a moment. "Just please don't tell me we have to walk to the clinic again."

James was standing next to the window. "We're in luck," he said, sounding amazed. "I can see your dad's Land Rover outside, Mandy!"

Mandy grabbed their coats and ran out into the street. Lauren followed close behind, holding Tarka carefully in her arms. Sure enough, Dr. Adam's car was rumbling over the snowpacked road in their direction.

"Dad!" Mandy called, waving her arms. "Over here!"

Dr. Adam stopped the Land Rover and rolled down the window. "I thought you might have come over here to check on Tarka," he said. "I got through my morning appointments early, so I thought I'd pay her a visit, too. How is she?"

Mandy told him about the smell coming from Tarka's cast.

Dr. Adam glanced at Lauren. "When did you first notice the smell?"

"I didn't," Lauren admitted, looking down at the snow-packed road. "Mandy did."

"OK," Dr. Adam said. "Hop in. I'll give you a lift back to the clinic."

Dr. Adam pushed open the passenger door and they all piled in. Lauren took the front seat, holding Tarka very gently on her lap.

"Any developments on Sesame?" Mandy asked her dad as the Land Rover bumped slowly along the road.

Dr. Adam shook his head. "I went to see the McFarlanes to give them an update before driving over to find you. There's been no change, I'm afraid."

After a careful journey back through the village, Dr. Adam swung into the driveway at Animal Ark. They carried Tarka inside, and Dr. Adam took her straight into a consulting room. The others followed closely.

"What happens if there *is* an infection?" Lauren asked Dr. Adam. Her voice sounded thin and strained. "You can treat it, can't you?"

"I hope so." Dr. Adam scrubbed his hands and pulled on a pair of surgical gloves. "But let's take a look first, shall we?" He carefully cut the plaster and peeled it away from Tarka's leg.

"So," Lauren persisted, "you only *hope* you can treat it. Are you saying that maybe you can't?"

Dr. Adam swabbed the wound with a piece of cotton, and Tarka flinched and pulled away. "The infection's pretty deep," he said, studying it. He looked up at Lauren with a serious expression on his face. "We need to start treating her with antibiotics at once, to avoid any risk of Tarka losing her leg."

Nine

Lauren turned so white that Mandy thought she was going to faint. James very quickly grabbed a chair and positioned it behind Lauren in case she needed to sit down.

"That's only the worst-case scenario," Dr. Adam said hastily, cleaning the wound in Tarka's leg as gently as he could. "Thanks to Mandy, it looks like we've caught it in time."

Wincing, Tarka looked up at Mandy with huge, soulful eyes. Mandy longed to pick her up and hug her. Biting her lip, she stroked Tarka's head while her father rebound the wound in a fresh dressing and attached a support splint for the broken bone. She stole a glance at Lauren, who still looked as white as a sheet.

"Luckily, we don't need electricity to treat infections," Dr. Adam told Lauren as he reached over to a drawer and pulled out a syringe. He took a handful of loose skin around Tarka's neck and inserted the needle. Tarka lay very still while he gave her the injection, and Mandy felt very proud of her for being so brave.

"We'll keep Tarka in the residential unit overnight and monitor her progress," Dr. Adam said. "Is that OK with you?"

Lauren swallowed. "I'll call Mom and tell her," she said. "Do you think the infection might get worse?"

Dr. Adam gave her an encouraging smile. "It shouldn't, now that we've started the antibiotics," he said, peeling off his surgical gloves. "Come on. Let's show Tarka where she'll be staying."

The unit was looking very festive, thanks to the efforts of Simon, the veterinary nurse. The walls and ceiling were draped in colorful tinsel and a little gas stove flickered merrily in one corner, keeping the room very cozy. Apart from Sesame's cage, the unit was empty.

Lauren called her mom to tell her that Tarka would be a guest at Animal Ark overnight. Just before they left the unit, Mandy checked on Sesame. The little bird was still sitting in the corner of his cage, his eyes closed and his food untouched. It wasn't look-ing good.

"I have to visit a farm up in the Dales," Dr. Adam said, as they returned to the clinic waiting room. "I'll be pass-ing your house, Lauren, if you want a lift."

"Can we have a ride, too, Dad?" Mandy asked quickly. "Just into the village. I want to go and talk to Mrs. McFarlane again about Sesame."

They all walked out to the Land Rover together. While she was waiting for the others to climb in, Mandy crunched the icy surface of the puddles with the heel of her boot, thinking hard about Sesame.

"Are you busy for the rest of the day, James?" she asked, when they were heading back into the village.

"I'm making your Christmas present this afternoon," James said, sounding a bit sheepish. "But I'm free until lunch."

Mandy made a couple of guesses. "What are you mak-ing? A chocolate cake?" she teased. "A space rocket? Give me a clue!"

James looked mysterious. "You'll have to wait and see," he said. "What do you want to do this morning?"

"I thought we could make a complete search of the post office, just in case the McFarlanes are missing a major clue about Sesame's illness," Mandy told him. "I really think it's our last hope."

Dr. Adam pulled up outside the post office.

"See you later, Lauren," said Mandy, as she and James got out.

Lauren just stared silently out of the Land Rover window. Mandy tried again. "I'm sure Tarka's going to be fine."

"Yeah," said Lauren sullenly. She still didn't look at Mandy.

"Come on," said James, tugging on Mandy's sleeve.

Mandy gazed at the Land Rover as it crunched away over the snow. What was going on inside Lauren's head? She really hoped Lauren wasn't giving up on Tarka for good. The gorgeous spaniel deserved to have everyone on her side!

In the warm, creamy light of a pair of oil lanterns on the post office counter, the little store looked even busier than the day before. Mandy sniffed the air. The lanterns gave off a strong smell of oil that took a little getting used to.

"The closer we get to Christmas, the more shopping people find they have to do," Mrs. McFarlane explained, pushing a lock of hair out of her eyes as she came over to greet Mandy and James. "I can't remember a busier year than this."

There was an unfamiliar *ker-ching* noise from behind the counter.

"Where did you get that, Mrs. McFarlane?" Mandy asked, staring in astonishment at the cumbersome, brown plastic cash register. Little numbers popped up at the top as Mr. McFarlane added up a customer's bill.

"We found it in the back," Mrs. McFarlane replied. "It must be nearly thirty years old, but it doesn't need electricity, thank goodness. Sometimes I wonder if we don't make things harder for ourselves these days than we have to. Do you have any more news on Sesame, Mandy?"

She looked so hopeful that Mandy couldn't voice her worst fears for the little bird. Avoiding the question, she asked instead, "Would it be all right if James and I take a look around the post office for clues, Mrs. McFarlane?"

The postmistress looked sad. "I guess you haven't found out what's wrong with him yet, then?"

Mandy shook her head. "No, we haven't," she said as gently as she could. "But we're not giving up yet, I promise."

Mrs. McFarlane looked a little more cheerful. "Perhaps two fresh pairs of eyes will see something that we missed," she said. "Go ahead. I'm afraid I won't be able to help much." She indicated the long line of customers. "We've got our hands full this morning, as you can see!"

There wasn't much stock left on the McFarlanes' shelves. Ignoring the nagging thought that someone might have bought the crucial piece of evidence in the form of a chewed laundry powder box or tube of glue and taken it away, Mandy turned over everything she could see on the shelves: cards, wrapping paper, soft toys, and the few remaining balls of wool, DVDs, and potted plants. Everything was intact.

"Nothing." James sighed, straightening up as they reached the last shelf. "Now what?"

Mandy gazed out the window, waiting for inspiration. The McFarlanes' Christmas tree decorations twinkled in the corner of her eye, winking and turning gently on their branches. Her eyes traveled up the tree, scanning every twirling robin and snowflake, bulb and angel — until they came to rest on the great golden star at the very top.

"James, go and ask the McFarlanes for their ladder," Mandy said urgently.

James brought the stepladder as quickly as he could. With her heart pounding, Mandy climbed to the very top and undid the wire that held the star to the highest branch. She turned the decoration over in her fingers. Now that she was up close, she was even more certain. It looked as if one point of the star had been nibbled by a very small, very busy beak! The gold paint was flaking off, showing the dull gleam of silvery metal beneath.

"I think we've got it," Mandy said, coming back down the ladder as fast as she dared. She showed James the

star. "Quick! Let's tell the McFarlanes what we've found, and take this star to the clinic!"

Back at Animal Ark twenty minutes later, Dr. Hope examined the star carefully by the light of the clinic window.

"Well?" Mandy asked, still out of breath from running all the way down the road. "What do you think, Mom?"

"I think," Dr. Hope said slowly, "that you may have found the culprit, Mandy. This star is very old isn't it?"

Mandy nodded. "Mrs. McFarlane remembers her grandmother telling her stories about it."

Dr. Hope turned the star over in her hands. "They used lead paint on decorations like this in the old days," she said. "If this contains lead, then it would explain Sesame's condition. Lead is extremely toxic, particularly to birds."

"Is there anything we can do?" Mandy gulped.

Dr. Hope was still turning the star over in her hands. "Yes, although an X-ray would have picked up traces of the lead paint in Sesame's gullet and we could have started treatment sooner. But let's look on the bright side, OK? You and James have done some great detective work here, and we may still be in time to help Sesame. Let's get him into the clinic and start the treatment right away."

In the residential unit, Mandy was pleased to see that Tarka was fast asleep. She hoped she was having lovely healing dreams, and reached through the bars of the cage to stroke the tip of Tarka's nose very gently. The spaniel twitched in her sleep, but her eyes remained closed. Mandy wondered if Lauren would visit later.

Sesame was still hunched in the corner of his cage. His feathers were even more ruffled up than before, and the bright blue color had lost some of its shine. Dr. Emily lifted the little bird out and carried him through to the clinic.

"I need some calcium editate, Mandy, to help Sesame break down the lead and pass it through his digestive system," she said, putting the bird on the table in one of the consulting rooms. "You'll find it in the store cupboard. Oh, and James? Could you get some peanut butter for me?"

James looked astonished. "Peanut butter?"

"Mom's going to mix some penicillamine drops in the peanut butter and give it to Sesame, aren't you, Mom?" Mandy guessed, handing over the calcium editate and a tiny syringe. She'd seen her parents do something similar with other sick birds that came to the clinic.

"That's right," Dr. Emily said, bending over the tiny bird. "Like calcium editate, penicillamine neutralizes the lead and helps the body to get rid of it naturally.

With the addition of peanut butter, it'll pass more quickly through Sesame's digestive system."

James got the peanut butter, and together, he and Mandy mixed a tiny amount with the drops Dr. Emily gave them. After Dr. Emily had injected the calcium editate directly into Sesame's chest muscle, they fed Sesame the liquefied peanut butter through a small dropper. The little bird lay quietly in Dr. Emily's hands as she massaged his body with her thumbs.

"We should know whether the treatment has been successful in a few hours," Dr. Emily said. "Jean?" she called to Jean Knox as she came out of the consulting room with Mandy and James hot on her heels. "Could you get a message to the McFarlanes for me and let them know that we've managed to treat Sesame for lead poisoning?"

"I'll do it right now," Jean Knox said promptly, putting down her pen and picking up the phone.

"The electricity's still off," Mandy pointed out as Jean frowned, perplexed, at the dead receiver. "Don't worry. James and I will go into the village later and tell them."

She glanced anxiously at the small, motionless bird in her mother's hands. Would Sesame pull through — or had the diagnosis come too late?

*   *   *

The next morning, the snow lay even thicker than it had the day before. There had been a fresh fall in the night, and the landscape looked fat and pristine again. Mandy lay in bed and blinked at the now-familiar white light that streamed in through her bedroom curtains. She realized she was starting to look forward to seeing green fields and gray stone walls again, when the snow melted. *If* the snow melted, she thought, getting dressed and hurrying downstairs. Sometimes it felt as if Welford would be blanketed in white forever.

Down in the kitchen, she was surprised to see her grandmother sitting at the kitchen table. She was looking very serious.

"Gran's got bad news." Dr. Emily sighed.

Mandy looked anxiously at her grandmother. "Smoky's OK, isn't he?" She couldn't bear it if another animal got sick this week — particularly if it was her grandparents' much-loved cat.

"Smoky's fine," said Dorothy Hope. "But unless they hurry up and fix the electricity in the village, it looks like we're going to have to cancel the Christmas dance. We were hoping to raise a large amount of money for the local hospital this year, too."

Mandy gasped. With all the drama surrounding Tarka and Sesame, she'd forgotten about the dance. "We can't cancel it!" she said. "We can get gas heaters in to keep the hall warm, and we could light candles around the hall. I'm sure everyone will still want to come!"

"It's not that, Mandy," said her grandmother. "It's the dance itself. With no electricity, the DJ won't be able to play any music. What's the point of a dance without music?"

Mandy sat down heavily. She hadn't thought of that. It was strange how she'd always taken electricity for granted — until now.

"I hate this snow!" she burst out.

Dorothy Hope looked surprised. "I thought you loved it."

"I did once." Mandy sighed. "But it just seems to cause trouble."

"Don't worry, sweetie," said Dr. Emily, resting her hand on Mandy's shoulder. "How about getting Lauren here for a sleepover? She called this morning on the cell phone to ask about Tarka — who's looking a little better, by the way. Lauren's mom stayed with her grandfather last night because of the weather, and she's now snowed in. So Lauren will be on her own tonight."

"Tarka's feeling better?" Mandy asked, brightening up. It was wonderful to hear that Lauren had called to ask about Tarka. Maybe Lauren was finally starting to see how fantastic Tarka really was.

"She ate a hearty breakfast this morning, so she's got

her appetite back," Dr. Emily reported. "But we'll keep an eye on her for a while longer. So how about it? Would you like to invite Lauren to stay tonight?"

"Sounds great, Mom," said Mandy, grabbing a piece of fire-cooked toast from the plate on the kitchen table. "Can I go see Tarka now?"

Dr. Emily called Lauren to invite her over as Mandy hurried through to the clinic to check on Tarka and bring her the good news that Lauren was coming to visit.

She was stopped short by a sharp *rat-a-tat* on the kitchen window.

"Mandy!" Dr. Adam banged on the window again. She could hardly see her dad's face through the folds of the enormous scarf he'd wrapped around his neck. "If I chop the firewood, could you give me a hand bringing it in?"

Chopping and toting the wood took longer than Mandy expected. As she staggered inside with the last armful of freshly split logs and dropped them in the wicker basket beside the fire, she heard the telltale sound of Bill's ATV roaring into the Animal Ark driveway. She ran around the side of the house to see Lauren climbing off the back of Bill's trailer.

"I'm so glad you're here," Mandy said, dragging Lauren inside as Bill handed over the mail and had a brief chat with Jean at the reception desk. "Animals heal more quickly when their owners are around. Tarka will be so pleased to see you."

Lauren bit her lip. "I doubt it," she said, unwinding her scarf.

"She will, you'll see," Mandy said confidently.

Tarka was awake when they entered the residential unit. As soon as she saw Lauren she started wagging her tail and trying to jump up against the sides of the cage.

Lauren smiled for the first time since she'd arrived. "Tarka's never done that for me before!" she said, bending down and stroking Tarka as Mandy opened up the cage.

"She always wanted to be your friend, Lauren," said Mandy, stroking Tarka's head. Tarka's nose still felt hot and drier than it should have been. Mandy tried not to worry as she scratched Tarka behind the ears.

"I guess she has." Lauren petted Tarka's throat and Tarka licked her again, showing her pleasure with little gruff noises at the back of her throat. "I feel like everything's been my fault. I should have known that Tarka was in pain with her hips, and I should have stopped her from jumping on that wall. I didn't even notice the infection until you came along. Some dog owner I am."

Her words came out in a rush, as if she couldn't wait

to get everything off her chest. Mandy felt very sorry for her.

"It's a normal reaction, Lauren," she said. "You're not a vet — no one expects you to notice medical stuff like hip dysplasia. The most important thing is that Tarka's getting the best treatment, and that you're here right now giving her lots of love."

Tarka squirmed with pleasure as Lauren talked to her and scratched her ears and chest. Then she glanced up and saw Sesame sitting quietly in his cage. "Is that the McFarlanes' parakeet?" she asked, getting up to take a look. "He's got the most gorgeous feathers, doesn't he? I'd love to have a couple for my set design. They'd look fabulous in a jar, like icy-blue ferns in the Snow Queen's palace."

"There may be a few on the bottom of the cage you could have," Mandy said, taking Sesame's water bottle and going to the sink in the corner to fill it up. "He's still pretty sick. We treated him for lead poisoning, and we're waiting to see if he passes anything out of his system. He hasn't been responding to the treatment as quickly as we'd like."

"Can I take him out of his cage?" Lauren asked.

"Sure," said Mandy. "Some company might cheer him up." She finished filling the water bottle and turned back to Lauren.

To her astonishment, she saw Sesame was already perching on Lauren's finger, his tiny claws gripping her tightly. "Sesame!" she exclaimed. "Lauren, you must have a healing touch. We really thought he'd given up!"

It looked like Sesame had passed some of the lead at last. Mandy checked the bottom of the cage for droppings, and was pleased to see that his system had clearly started to get rid of the poisonous paint.

Sesame gave a brief whistle and moved his little feet along Lauren's finger. Lauren laughed and stroked the bird's blue back with delight.

"It's good to know I've got the healing talent." She grinned. Looking serious for a moment, she added, "Let's hope it works on Tarka, too, right?"

That evening, the fire flickered cozily in the grate as Mandy and Lauren settled down after supper. Two sleeping bags lay on the floor in front of the hearth, with Tarka fast asleep beside them on an old, folded comforter. After much cajoling, Mandy had persuaded her parents to let them have Tarka in the living room with them that evening. "She loves people," she had explained, "and the company will do her good. Now that Lauren's taking an interest in Tarka, don't you think this is a good chance for them to bond?" As it wouldn't directly interfere with Tarka's treatment, her mom and dad had agreed.

Lauren was rummaging in her backpack for her mom's Christmas stocking. "I thought I could finish the details tonight," she said, as Tarka sniffed at the bundle of rainbow-colored wool. "And I've got a surprise for you, Mandy." She laid down her knitting, which definitely looked like an oversized stocking now, and went back to her bag for something else.

"I've got one for you, too." Mandy grinned. "Look!"

Tarka had nosed her way inside the stocking, which was just roomy enough for a small plump spaniel. The sides of the stocking bulged as Tarka turned around until her face was peeping out of the open end, then flopped down with her head on her paws.

"Tarka!" Lauren gasped. "That's Mom's stocking!"

Tarka's little black-and-gray muzzle peeped out adorably from the stocking's mouth and the back end of the stocking started twitching as she wagged her tail. Mandy couldn't help laughing at Lauren's expression.

"Honestly," Lauren groaned, scratching Tarka's ears. "I can't leave her alone for five minutes, can I?"

"Oh, you have to let Tarka stay in there!" Mandy begged. "She looks so cozy. It's like a perfect doggie sleeping bag! It's even got all those dog motifs on it."

"She does look very cute," Lauren admitted. "And it'll

keep her really warm, just like your dad advised." Tarka wagged her tail harder so that the toe of the stocking flapped against the floor. "All that work," Lauren sighed. Mandy noticed a twinkle in her eye. "Go on then, Tarka. It's yours. I'm sure Mom will understand."

Mandy grinned as Lauren tousled the spaniel's ears. It was such a relief to see Lauren bonding with Tarka at last.

"Now, back to that surprise," said Lauren, reaching inside her bag again. "You know you said you wanted to knit, Mandy?" she asked over her shoulder.

"Yes!" said Mandy.

Lauren pulled out two balls of royal blue wool and a pair of knitting needles, and waved them at Mandy in triumph. "Well, your first lesson starts right here," she said, passing the needles to Mandy.

The first thing Lauren showed her was how to hold the needles and loop the wool around it to begin. She'd brought a simple pattern for a pair of socks with her, and helped Mandy cast on the first row of stitches.

"I've just realized!" Mandy exclaimed. "I've been making these special Christmas pictures for everyone this week, Lauren, but I couldn't think of the right picture for James. But now I can stop trying. He told me the other day that what he really needed was socks!"

"Well, you'd better get cracking," said Lauren. "You've only got two days left."

Mandy struggled with the first few rows, but soon got the hang of it. Following her instructions very carefully and turning to Lauren for advice every now and then, she'd soon knitted something that looked faintly sock-like. As they knitted companionably together, Mandy found that they were talking about all kinds of things. They discussed Tarka's hip dysplasia, and in the absence of the Internet, Mandy went and got one of her dad's reference books and went through the symptoms and treatment with Lauren. The older girl was genuinely interested, and Mandy was delighted to think that she was helping her to understand Tarka's condition.

At last the fire faded to glowing embers, and the girls got ready for bed. They let Tarka out into the yard, then brought her inside before she got too cold. The spaniel went straight over to her doggy stocking and snuggled inside.

"I hope my sleeping bag is as cozy as that one," Lauren remarked. She lay down in her own bag and wiggled over until she could put her arm around Tarka.

Mandy put the half-knitted socks carefully on a chair, and smiled to herself as she watched Tarka pressing closer to Lauren. For those two at least, it really did look like the perfect Christmas ending.

Ten

Mandy yawned and rubbed her eyes as she sat up. She couldn't think where she was at first. Then she saw Lauren and Tarka asleep on the floor next to her, and the familiar living-room drapes. Her fledgling socks lay on the sofa next to the fireplace.

Wriggling out of her sleeping bag, Mandy padded to the window and stared outside. The snow looked a little thinner today, with blades of grass poking through here and there. She felt oddly relieved.

"Breakfast's on the table!" Mandy's mom called through the door.

At the sound of Dr. Emily's voice, Lauren opened her

eyes. Tarka gave a protesting whine as she sat up. "Breakfast? I'm starving!" she said eagerly. "Mmm, do I smell oatmeal?"

"Best thing in this weather," declared Mandy's dad as the girls came into the kitchen. "It's as good as a woolly lining in your boots."

Mandy glanced at the saucepan of water bubbling on the little gas stove. "Still no electricity?" she guessed.

Dr. Emily poured hot water into four mugs, trying not to spill too much. "No." She sighed, putting the saucepan down and staring, annoyed, at the puddle of water on the table. "I never thought I could miss a kettle this much."

Mandy remembered her grandmother's bad news yesterday. Her heart sank as she asked, "Do you think the dance will definitely be canceled now?"

"It certainly looks that way," said Dr. Emily.

Mandy's disappointed silence was broken as Tarka limped into the kitchen and gave a brief woof.

"Hungry?" Dr. Adam raised his eyebrows as he bent down to scratch the old spaniel's back. "That's a good sign. After breakfast, we'll take a look at that infection, old girl."

Mandy bent down and stroked Tarka's neck. Surreptitiously, she felt the spaniel's nose. It was definitely cooler and damper than yesterday. All Tarka had needed to get better was to know that Lauren really loved her. Feeling suddenly optimistic again, Mandy helped clear the table, then dashed off to wash and dress for the day. The dance might be canceled, but it looked as if Tarka was on the mend!

Dr. Adam's inspection of Tarka's leg confirmed Mandy's hopes.

"Much better," he said, applying a new dressing to the spaniel's leg. "I think we can replace that cast today."

Tarka was a model of patience as Dr. Adam replastered her broken leg, even wagging her tail briefly as Mandy and Lauren stood by her head and took turns stroking her ears.

"I think this calls for a celebration," Dr. Adam declared, lifting Tarka down before peeling off his gloves and ushering Mandy and Lauren back into the waiting room. He reached up for a cupboard high over his head, and pulled out a bulging wool sock. "Santa's come a couple of days early this year," he said with a smile, as he handed the sock to Lauren.

The sock had a label addressed to Tarka, just like a Christmas stocking. Laughing, Lauren tipped the contents onto the counter. There were some glucosamine tablets, a sturdy retractable leash, some low-fat dog treats, and a hot-water bottle with a fleecy cover for Tarka to sleep with on cold nights.

"Looks like Santa takes Tarka's health and fitness as seriously as we do." Dr. Emily grinned, putting her head around the door of her consulting room.

There was a scrunching sound of wheels on the snow outside and the slam of a car door. Moments later, Vanessa Morley stepped into the clinic.

"Mom!" Lauren ran to the clinic door and gave her mother a hug. Tarka rolled on her back with delight as Vanessa bent down to rub her tummy.

"Someone's feeling better." Vanessa laughed as Tarka squirmed blissfully beneath her fingers. She looked up at Lauren. "Grandpa's feeling better, too, I'm happy to say."

"Where did you get the car, Mom?" Lauren asked.

"I borrowed it from one of Grandpa's neighbors," said Vanessa. "Thank goodness the road was a little clearer! It's still blocked between here and Walton, though. Come on, let's get you two home."

Mandy helped Lauren to pack up her things. "Thanks for the knitting lesson," she said, as Lauren brushed down Tarka's Christmas stocking and tucked it into her bag.

"I should be thanking *you*," Lauren said, shouldering

her bag and smiling at Mandy. "I can't believe I never realized how sweet Tarka was before. Now, promise you'll finish those socks, Mandy. There's nothing more useless than half-finished knitting."

"I don't have much choice," Mandy pointed out with a smile. "I don't have anything else for James's Christmas present!" She knelt down and planted a kiss on Tarka's warm, graying muzzle. Then she followed the Morleys out to the car and helped Lauren to lift Tarka into the back, where a warm dog bed was waiting for her. Waving vigorously, she watched the Morleys swing out of the driveway and away in a swirl of powdery snow.

When James arrived that afternoon, he found Mandy and her mom in the residential unit.

"How's Sesame?" he asked, peering over Dr. Emily's shoulder as Mandy eased the little bird out of his cage.

"Much better." Mandy planted a kiss on Sesame's soft, downy head and the parakeet chirped weakly at her.

"So much better that he can go home today," said Dr. Emily, getting a small cardboard carrier. "In fact, I was hoping that you two might be able to take him back this afternoon. Do you have any plans?"

Mandy and James shook their heads. "Not really," said Mandy. "Lauren called to say her model stage set was finished, if we wanted to come over and look."

Dr. Emily sighed. "Ah, stage sets," she said dreamily. "When I was a girl, I loved the ballet, you know. I went to see *The Nutcracker* one Christmas Eve — everything glittered and sparkled on that stage. It was very magical."

Mandy thought of the excitement she'd felt at the Christmas show, seeing the brightly painted backdrops and beautiful velvet curtains. She knew just what her mother meant.

"We need to line Sesame's box with newspaper," she

said, taking the carrier from her mother, who was still gazing misty-eyed as she thought about ballet-filled memories.

"I'll get some old papers from the living room," James offered.

Remembering the half-knitted socks lying on the armchair, Mandy leaped in front of him. "Um, I'll do it," she said quickly. "You can get some food, James."

James looked puzzled. "Whatever," he said with a shrug.

Mandy hurried into the living room and gathered lots of newspaper. She hid the half-finished socks under a sofa cushion in case James came in later, and then returned to the clinic where James was filling a small plastic bowl with birdseed.

After Mandy had tucked plenty of newspaper into the corners of the box, they put the parakeet inside and gently closed the lid. Sesame's chirping stopped abruptly.

"I hope he's OK in there," said James as they picked their way down the snowy road, taking turns carrying the box. "He's gotten very quiet."

"When it's dark, birds think it's bedtime," Mandy reminded him, "remember? He's probably wondering why he doesn't feel sleepy even though the lights have gone out!"

"Speaking of lights," said James, "I hear the dance has been canceled."

"I know." Mandy sighed. "Grandma's already been around the village putting 'canceled' stickers on the posters."

"It's a real shame," said James. "Maybe we could have an evening of games and contests, or do a show by candlelight instead."

They pushed open the door of the post office.

"Mandy!" Mrs. McFarlane hurried over, looking hopeful. "Is that . . . ?"

Mandy smiled in reply and put the carrier on the counter. She opened the top, and they all peered inside. Sesame pulled his head from beneath his wing and blinked at them, looking annoyed, as if he had only just fallen asleep.

Mrs. McFarlane lifted the bird gently from the box and held him up to her face. "My, don't you look better! You need a good sesame-seed dinner, I think." She carried the bird to his cage where a bowl of nothing but sesame seeds was waiting for him. "Please thank your parents for us, Mandy. We've grown very attached to this little guy, even though we haven't had him for long."

As they left the post office and headed for Lauren's house, Mandy glanced at James. "What did you say about a show a little while ago?" she asked.

"Oh, nothing," said James. "It would be impossible, anyway. I mean, we could decorate the hall and everything like an ice cave, like you said at the committee meeting, but we'd never have time to rehearse. No, it has to be a dance or nothing."

An idea was beginning to form in Mandy's mind. "Ice cave," she murmured, staring up the road at Lauren's wreath-decorated front door. "The Snow Queen's palace. I wonder . . . ?"

"Mandy, a show's impossible," James began.

"I know," Mandy said, knocking on the Morleys' door. "I wasn't thinking of doing one. Like you say, it's a dance or nothing."

It was difficult to tell who was more pleased to see them, Lauren or Tarka. The old spaniel did her best to frisk around Mandy's and James's feet as Lauren showed them her finished stage set design with pride. Mandy smiled when she saw how close Tarka was pressing against Lauren's legs. She always knew that Tarka loved Lauren as much as she loved Lauren's mom.

"It's wonderful!" Mandy knelt down to examine the intricately detailed theater set. "Uh, how difficult would it be to re-create all these decorations in full-size?"

"It's not as difficult as it looks," Lauren said. "Full-scale, it would just be a matter of draping the walls in white and silver fabrics and hanging big cutout snowflakes from the ceiling. You could use wire coat hangers and white or silver Christmas ornaments for the chandelier instead of paper clips; spray-paint some chicken wire silver and bend it into some interesting shapes for the backdrop and the columns — and voilà! The Snow Queen's palace, come to life."

Over chocolate chip cookies, she showed Mandy and James the model figures she'd made out of pipe cleaners. The Snow Queen was wearing a magnificent ruff — "A doily," Lauren revealed with a grin — and her courtiers wore coats and helmets of aluminum foil.

"It's incredible what you can do with a little household stuff, isn't it?" said James.

Mandy thoughtfully turned one of the aluminum-foil courtiers over in her hand. If she made a few calls to the committee tonight on her mom's cell, maybe Welford's Christmas dance wouldn't have to be canceled after all.

On Christmas Eve, the snow outside Mandy's bedroom window was looking considerably patchier, with plants and shrubs clearly visible around the edge of the lawn.

"It's weird, but I'm pleased the snow is melting before Christmas," Mandy confessed over breakfast. "I'd almost forgotten how nice green grass looked."

"Nothing weird about that," said Dr. Adam, spreading a generous dollop of marmalade on his fire-cooked toast. "The grass is always greener on the other side, as it were."

Mandy groaned at her dad's awful pun.

"Julian Hardy called this morning before you came down, Mandy," said Dr. Emily. "I take it he's the last committee member you had to speak to about your new plans for the Christmas dance?"

Mandy nodded. "What did he think?" she asked.

"He loves the idea," said Dr. Emily, "but he said it all depends on getting some live music. And that won't be easy at such short notice."

"Grandma thinks we can do it," Mandy said, pushing back her chair and taking her bowl to the sink.

"Your grandmother thinks anything is possible, particularly when her hospital fund-raising is involved." Dr. Adam grinned.

"Leave it to me," Mandy said, kissing her parents. "I've got to make one house call this morning, and it'll all be fixed." She crossed her fingers on both hands before she took down her coat and put it on.

"Good luck!" her dad called as she pushed open the front door and set off for the village.

The wind was sharper than ever although there

weren't any snowflakes; there would be a hard freeze tonight. Mandy hurried as fast as she could through the snow, her mind full of possibilities. If Lauren's mom said yes, Welford could end up with the best Christmas dance they'd ever had. She practiced her skating on the puddles all the way up to the crossroads, down Main Street and down Lauren's road, throwing in the odd pirouette when the ice was strong enough to take it.

"Hi," she puffed when Lauren opened her front door. "Thanks for letting me come over this morning. I've got a huge favor to ask." She bent down and petted Tarka who whined with pleasure, wagging tail into a blur.

Vanessa Morley was in the living room, practicing playing her guitar. She smiled as Mandy came in with Lauren and Tarka. "You sounded eager on the phone," she said. "Sit down, Mandy. What's up?"

Tarka limped to her Christmas stocking by the flickering fire and wriggled into it with a sigh of contentment. "Tarka looks really at home in her stocking," said Mandy, sitting down on the sofa.

Lauren beamed. "It's great, isn't it? I was thinking of knitting a few more for next Christmas, and seeing if the McFarlanes would be able to sell them in their store."

"That's a great idea," Mandy said. "I'll ask my parents if they could sell some at the clinic, too!"

The girls grinned at each other, and Tarka wagged her tail again, making the toe of the stocking jump around.

"Now, down to business," said Mandy, looking at Lauren and her mother. "You know how we've been planning a Christmas dance at the village hall tonight? Well, we were going to cancel it because the DJ can't play music without electricity. But then I had this fantastic idea. And Lauren, if you could help, too, that would be awesome."

"And the idea is?" Vanessa prompted.

"To have a live music event, decorated with Lauren's stage set design," Mandy said. "It would be totally Christmassy with all the silver and white — and I wondered if there was any way you could help with the music, Vanessa. Lauren mentioned once before that you had a lot of experience playing at festivals."

"It would be fantastic!" Lauren said, her eyes glowing at the thought of turning her stage set into a full-scale creation. "We could use white sheets for the walls, and we've got lots of wire coat hangers and ornaments for the chandeliers."

"James's dad has lots of stuff in his toolshed," Mandy said, thrilled by Lauren's enthusiasm. "He might have rolls of chicken wire we could spray and twist into columns for the dance floor. Some of the details might be tricky, but the basic idea would be there!"

"Tonight?" said Vanessa, setting aside her guitar. "It's pretty short notice, Mandy."

Mandy felt crestfallen. "I know," she said. "But I thought it was worth asking."

"Pretty short notice," Vanessa repeated with a twinkle in her eye, "given that I was having the band over for dinner tonight and I've already made the casserole."

Mandy blinked. "Does that mean the band's going to be in Welford, anyway?"

"Yep," said Vanessa. "And given that we usually end up playing together after supper, what better than playing for the whole village?"

Mandy felt dizzy. This was better than she had hoped! "You mean it?" she asked at last.

Vanessa nodded. "After all you did for Tarka, it's the least I can do. Just tell us when to show up!"

Mandy ran home, tearing the "canceled" stickers off the posters and writing "still on — with a twist!" in big black letters right across the middle, using a big black marker she'd borrowed from Lauren. She felt as if she could fly all the way back to Animal Ark if she jumped high enough.

Bouncing up the steps to the clinic, she burst through the door.

"Guess what!" she cried. She paused and stared at

Mrs. McFarlane, who was sitting in the waiting room. "Hello," she said, frowning. "Is everything OK with Sesame?"

Mrs. McFarlane rubbed her reddened eyes. "Your mom and dad are examining him right now," she said. "They said it would be better if I stayed out here — they'll let me know if . . . if . . . Oh, Mandy! Sesame got much worse today. I think he might die!"

Eleven

Mandy rushed into the consulting room. "Mom, Dad!" she gasped. "What happened?"

"Good to see you, Mandy," said her dad, bending over the little bird. "We're going to need your help. This little fellow is fighting for his life."

"But I thought Sesame was better," Mandy whispered.

"Unfortunately lead poisoning isn't as simple as that," said Dr. Emily. "The poisoning can occur at different stages as the lead is absorbed by the stomach lining. We were hoping that he'd managed to pass most of the lead out of his system already, but Mrs. McFarlane told us that he suddenly went rigid today and fell off his perch.

Take this flashlight and angle it at Sesame, would you? We need all the light we can get for this operation."

"You're going to operate?" Mandy couldn't believe it. Her mother took down a bottle of anesthetic and fit a tiny rubber mask to the nozzle.

"We have no choice," said Dr. Adam, riffling through his surgical instruments for an endoscopy tube small enough to pass down the tiny bird's throat. "It's too late to hope that Sesame will pass the rest of the lead on his own. We have to remove the metal ourselves. Hold that light steady now."

Mandy gripped the heavy flashlight tightly as her mother fit the rubber mask around Sesame's beak. Anesthetizing small birds was tricky; Mandy knew that if her mother gave Sesame too much anesthetic, he might not wake up. Once Sesame was asleep, Dr. Adam threaded the endoscopy tube down the parakeet's throat, then passed a very tiny pair of forceps down the tube. He worked steadily, moving the forceps carefully a step at a time. Every now and then, he pulled the forceps out and deposited a sliver of lead paint in a dish. The minutes ticked by — five, ten . . .

"Two more minutes," Dr. Emily murmured. "We can't anesthetize a bird this size for any longer than that, Adam."

"Almost there," Mandy's dad replied, twisting the

forceps around. "I can see just one more fragment —
there, got it!"

As he dropped the particle of lead paint in the dish,
Dr. Emily carefully removed the rubber mask from
Sesame's beak. Mandy's hand was trembling as she held
the flashlight and watched her father remove the endoscopy tube.

After an agonizing thirty seconds, the little bird's
eyelids flickered.

"Welcome back, little fellow," said Dr. Adam, running
his fingertip over the top of Sesame's head. "Now we
just wait and see if we've been successful. Mandy, could
you get a cage ready for Sesame in the residential unit?
Your mom and I need to speak to Mrs. McFarlane."

Mandy gave Mrs. McFarlane her most encouraging
smile as she left the consulting room. Her legs seemed
to have turned to a mixture of Jell-O and string. After
the exhilaration of the revived dance plans, she felt as if
she'd been hit by a truck.

She scattered fresh sawdust in the birdcage and was
filling a water bottle when her parents came into the
unit with Mrs. McFarlane, who was holding Sesame as
if he were made of glass.

"Sesame will be warm and safe in here," Dr. Emily
told Mrs. McFarlane, gently taking the bird from her.
"We'll know how he is in a few hours."

Mrs. McFarlane nodded. "I have to get back," she said. "Mr. McFarlane's holding down the fort, and I can't leave him alone any longer."

"Do you think Sesame's going to die?" Mandy asked her mother when Mrs. McFarlane had left.

Her mom shook her head. "It's too early to say, but we mustn't give up hope. So, what happened at the Morleys'?"

Mandy found it hard to put aside her concern for Sesame. "Vanessa's going to bring her band," she said. "And Lauren's going to help decorate the hall. I said I'd meet her there at twelve o'clock. There's a lot to do."

"That's wonderful!" Dr. Emily checked her watch. "It's already ten to twelve," she said. "You'd better get ready."

Mandy stared at her mother. "I can't go out now," she said. "Not until we know if Sesame's going to be OK."

"But there's nothing you can do, Mandy," Dr. Emily reminded her.

"I can be here," Mandy insisted. "I'll be in my room. Will you call me if there's any change?"

When her mom nodded, Mandy trudged upstairs, thoughts of Sesame and the McFarlanes going around and around in her head. She took down her Christmas project folder. She had one more Christmas picture to do. Hoping it might take her mind off Sesame, she sat down and stared at the white piece of card stock, the paintbrush poised in her hand. Then, with a brisk shake of her head, she got to work.

Every half hour, Mandy went downstairs to check on Sesame's progress. And every time, her parents shook their heads: no change. The clock downstairs chimed the hour — one, two, three.

At three-thirty, Mandy took her finished Christmas paintings downstairs, checking to make sure her parents weren't in the kitchen. She carried them outside and laid them on the ground beside the bicycle shed. There was enough cover here to protect the pictures if it snowed or rained in the night — and just as important, they couldn't be seen from the house.

"Mandy!" Dr. Emily called out of the kitchen door. "Are you out there?"

Mandy flew inside. "Sesame?"

"It's OK." Her mom caught Mandy by the shoulders. "Sesame's come through the worst. He's going to be fine."

Mandy ran to the residential unit, where her father was hunkered down beside Sesame's cage. The little bird let out a feeble squeak when he saw Mandy. Laughing, she fell to her knees and put her face to

Sesame's cage. "You gave us quite a scare this morning," she said.

Sesame fluttered his wings at her.

"I'll tell the McFarlanes the good news right away," Mandy declared. "I've got to go into the village, anyway, to get ready for the dance. There's a hall to decorate!"

"At last!" Lauren exclaimed as Mandy ran into the hall. She was attaching swags of white and pale blue bedsheets to the walls with a terrifying-looking stapler.

"We'd almost given up on you," said James, emerging from underneath one of the silver-draped buffet tables. "Where have you been?"

"Emergency operation," Mandy gasped. Between puffs she managed to tell Lauren and James the good news about Sesame. "I came as fast as I could," she finished, glancing around the hall. "What can I do?"

"Anything!" Lauren begged. "The dance kicks off at six, and it's already four o'clock!"

Mandy started by putting candles inside the dozens of glass jelly jars brought by her grandmother. She placed them evenly around the hall, and lined them up along the stage where Vanessa's band would be performing.

"Hold the ladder, will you, Mandy?" Her grandfather

looked down from the top of a wobbly-looking step-ladder. "I've just got to put this in place." He waved a football-sized bunch of mistletoe and holly at Mandy.

"It looks fantastic, Grandpa," Mandy told him as he fixed it to the ceiling with a piece of silver ribbon.

"Beware anyone caught beneath it," Tom Hope joked, climbing down. "They'll be in for a very big kiss."

James, who was approaching with a mountain of tupperware boxes balanced in his arms, stopped in his tracks and walked backward as quickly as he could.

The hall filled with talking and laughter as the committee members and their families worked to transform the village hall into the Snow Queen's Palace. Lauren had made a magnificent coat-hanger chandelier to hang above the dance floor, while Dorothy Hope organized a line of helpers to bring in countless containers of food from the van parked outside to the silver-draped banquet tables.

"Is it OK if we come and warm up?" Vanessa Morley appeared at the door of the hall, with three men and a woman behind her. Tarka limped beside her, sniffing the food smells with excitement. Mandy was fascinated to see that one of the men carried a long, thin case that didn't fit any instrument she knew. She couldn't imagine what it might contain.

"Actually, we'd all like to warm up," Julian Hardy

remarked, squeezing past them with a box of lemonade bottles. "The gas heaters are taking forever to heat this place!"

Lauren ran over and crouched down to greet Tarka. "We'll put you in the utility room so you don't get stepped on," she told the spaniel, who wagged her tail happily. "Mandy, is it warm enough in there for her?"

Mandy nodded. "Blackie's already there, with a gas heater of his very own," she said.

Vanessa produced Tarka's Christmas stocking. "Put her in this, and she'll be toasty!" She passed it to Lauren, who headed for the utility room with Tarka at her heels.

Mandy continued swagging and hanging, stapling and spray-painting huge pieces of chicken wire as the Cloud Dancers climbed onto the stage and set up their instruments. She stopped mid-staple as the man unlocked the large instrument case.

"What *is* that?" she asked, staring at the enormously long, brown, wooden tube that was emerging.

"It's a didgeridoo," Lauren explained. "Colin learned to play it in Australia. It's the funkiest sound you've ever heard."

"Food coming through!" Dorothy Hope bustled past with yet another plate full of sandwiches.

"How much food is your grandmother bringing?" James asked.

"Enough to feed an army, as usual." Mandy grinned, helping her grandmother find space for the plate on the crowded table.

The hall was really beginning to feel magical, especially as daylight faded and the candles were lit. With a thrill of delight, Mandy realized that people were gathering outside, peering through the windows at their icy decorations.

"One, two, three . . ." Vanessa struck up a tune on her guitar and the band followed suit. A lively jig with guitar, drum, flute, and the didgeridoo soon set the committee members' feet tapping as the finishing touches were made to the hall.

"All done!" said Lauren at last, collapsing in a chair with a sigh of relief. "What do you think?"

The hall looked more beautiful than Mandy could ever remember. Lauren's coat-hanger chandelier hung proudly beside Tom Hope's mistletoe ball, the silvered chicken-wire columns spiraled up to the ceiling, the tables groaned with food, and the silver-and-white walls gleamed in the candlelight. "It's magnificent," she told Lauren. "I feel like I'm in fairyland!"

Julian Hardy clapped his hands. "Time to let in the hordes!" he declared.

Mandy watched as the revelers streamed into the hall with *oohs* and *aahs* of appreciation. Vanessa's band soon had people dancing, and the atmosphere couldn't have been more festive.

"Well, well!" Dr. Adam stepped through the doors and stared in wonder at the decorations.

"You've done a fantastic job," Dr. Emily said warmly, giving Mandy a hug.

"It's all Lauren's work," Mandy said, taking her parents' coats. "Go and see Gran. She's dying for you to see the food table before people start eating."

"Good old Dad," remarked Dr. Adam. "Trust him to be up there dancing."

Grandpa Hope, who was jigging merrily on the dance floor with Sara Hardy, raised a hand in greeting.

"Come here a minute, Mandy!" said James, appearing beside her. "I've got your Christmas present out back."

Mandy followed him to the utility room, where Blackie lay on his dog bed and Tarka was curled snugly in her stocking. Both dogs thumped their tails happily as Mandy and James bent down to give them a pet.

"Your grandfather thought Tarka in the stocking was the cutest thing he'd ever seen," said James with a grin, tickling Tarka's ears. Tarka wriggled blissfully in her stocking. "He took Tarka's picture, and says he wants to use it on the front cover of the next village newsletter!"

Mandy took the spaniel's warm head between her

hands and planted a kiss on her muzzle. "I can't think of anything nicer," she said.

James cleared his throat. "Your Christmas present is back here," he said, leading Mandy to the back door of the hall. "Sorry — it's a bit wobbly."

Mandy stared at the bird feeder that was propped up in the snow. It had a pitched roof, a wide feeding platform, and a big red bow tied around its post. It would look fantastic outside the kitchen window, and she'd be able to watch wild birds all year round. "You made this?" she said in amazement. "James, it's amazing!"

James blushed. "Thanks."

Mandy remembered her present for James. She dug down in her coat pocket and produced the socks with a flourish. "Here's yours!" she announced. "I'm sorry I didn't have time to wrap them, but with Sesame's illness and decorating the hall, I ran out of time. Lauren showed me how to knit," she added.

Looking doubtful, James took the socks and studied them. "Do I put them on my hands or feet?" he said at last.

Mandy whacked him playfully on the arm. "Good and thick, just like you said you needed."

James's face cleared. "Thanks, Mandy," he said gratefully. "They look as cozy as Tarka's stocking. But I thought you were doing pictures for everyone this year?"

"I made pictures for everyone else," Mandy explained.

"How did they turn out?" James asked, tucking his socks into his pocket.

"I don't know yet," said Mandy. "I have to wait until tomorrow to see if my secret plan has worked. Come on, let's go back inside. The party's only just beginning!"

The evening passed in a gleaming whirl of music and food and softly shining silver walls. Mandy danced until her feet ached, popping into the utility room every now and then to check on the dogs and, in particular, to make sure that Tarka was keeping away from any drafts. More often than not, Lauren was in there, too, giving Tarka a few low-fat dog treats and making sure she was comfortable.

As Mandy emerged from the utility room for the third time, there was an odd buzzing sound from overhead, and the hall's fluorescent strip lights flickered on. In the shock of the bright light, everyone stopped dancing and shielded their eyes.

"The power's back!" Mandy gasped.

Everyone cheered and hugged one another in the brightness. Then there was a pause.

"Should we turn the lights off and keep dancing?" Dr. Adam suggested, looking around the room.

"My thoughts exactly!" Grandpa Hope said promptly, reaching over for the light switch and flipping it off.

The hall returned to magical candlelight, and the dancing resumed. Dr. Emily, looking hot and out of breath, came to Mandy and put an arm around her shoulders. "At least we won't have to barbecue the turkey tomorrow," she pointed out. "Come on, Mandy. Come and dance!"

On Christmas Day, Mandy woke up very early. Resisting the urge to peek in her Christmas stocking, which felt fat and scrunchy and exciting on the end of her bed, she got up and pulled on her robe and slippers. Then, tiptoeing downstairs, she opened the kitchen door and stared outside.

The freezing cold had left a shimmer of frost over everything Mandy could see: the trees, the shed, the path, and the car. There was still plenty of snow on the hills, looking hard and shiny in the sunlight. Mandy rubbed her hands together. Perfect conditions for the sledding race she had promised James later! Suddenly, she was pleased to have a white Christmas after all.

Crunching through the patchy snow, she found her Christmas paintings beside the shed where she had left them the day before.

The pictures sparkled in the crisp morning light, frosty swirls lighting up the snowy hills, snowmen, snowflakes, and mountains that Mandy had painted. The frost gave all the pictures a chilly, magical quality — and it was all the more special knowing that the frost wouldn't last for long. Carrying the pictures carefully back to the house, Mandy strung them up outside the kitchen window so that the ice crystals wouldn't melt too quickly. They would be the first things her parents saw when they came downstairs.

Then she skipped back inside the house and admired her work through the window. The frost pictures looked even better than she had hoped!

There was a heavy-looking present sitting on the kitchen table, with a tag that read, MERRY CHRISTMAS, MANDY! WITH ALL OUR LOVE, MOM AND DAD. Mandy picked it up. It was the same shape as the package her dad had been so worried about earlier in the week. *So*, Mandy thought, a thrill going through her, *it wasn't veterinary supplies after all!*

Carefully peeling off the wrapping paper, she opened it and gasped. Nestling in a bed of bubblewrap and tissue paper lay a pair of shiny white ice skates.

Mandy hugged them to her and dashed upstairs. "Merry Christmas, Mom and Dad!" she called, taking the stairs two at a time. "Merry Christmas!"

ABOUT THE AUTHOR

Ben Baglio was born in New York, and grew up in a small town in southern New Jersey. He was the only boy in a family with three sisters.

Ben spent a lot of his childhood reading. English was always his favorite subject, and after graduating from high school, he went on to study English Literature at the University of Pennsylvania. During his coursework, he was able to spend a year in Edinburgh, Scotland.

After graduation, Ben worked as a children's book editor in New York City. He also wrote his first book, which was about the Olympics in ancient Greece. Five years later, he took a job at a publishing house in England.

Ben is the author of the Dolphin Diaries series, and is perhaps most well known for the Animal Ark and Animal Ark Hauntings series. These books were originally published in England (under the pseudonym Lucy Daniels), and have since gone on to be published in the U. S., and translated into 15 languages.

Aside from writing, Ben enjoys scuba diving and swimming, music and movies. He has a beagle named Bob, who is by his side whenever he writes.